DO NOT REMOVE
CARDS FROM POCKET

KEVIN O'CONNOR

A N D

THE LIGHT BRIGADE

By LEONARD WIBBERLEY

———————

ARIEL BOOKS / NEW YORK

FARRAR, STRAUS AND CUDAHY

Ariel Books
is a division of
Farrar, Straus & Cudahy, Inc.

Published simultaneously in Canada by
Ambassador Books, Ltd., Toronto.
Manufactured in the U. S. A.
American Book–Stratford Press, Inc., New York

AUTHOR'S NOTE

In writing this story, I have deliberately selected a regiment—the 10th Hussars—which took no part in the Charge of the Light Brigade. I did this so that no one will come to the conclusion, quite unwarranted, that the officers of the regiment depicted in this book are drawn from real persons.

The best book I've read on the Charge of the Light Brigade is Cecil Woodham-Smith's *The Reason Why*. Since I do not agree with what seems to be a majority opinion that young Americans are confined in their reading ability to eight-word sentences, I strongly recommend *The Reason Why* to them, and rejoice in the fact that *this* sentence contains nearly fifty words.

LEONARD WIBBERLEY

CHAPTER ONE

TOM OF THE THREE FINGERS came over the top of Spaniard's Hill one morning and made his way slowly towards where I was working on our potato patch outside our cabin in County Galway, Ireland. It was the autumn of 1853 and myself, Kevin O'Connor, was seventeen years of age at the time, but grown as big as any man. I'd been working hard since dawn, digging the first potato crop (the second and main crop would not be taken up until December) and paused to watch Tom as he walked towards me.

Tom was a tinker—some said a gypsy and some said a heathen. He tramped the whole of Ireland, year in and year out, mending pots and pans and kettles where such work was to be found, and playing tunes on his fiddle for food and shelter when there was no tinkering to be done. Despite the fact that he was missing a finger of his right hand, he played with great ability.

To hear Tom talk you'd believe that he knew every man in Ireland from the English lord lieutenant in his castle in Dublin to the last sailor to

1

get off a ship in Galway Bay. A wizened little monkey of a man he was, with brown eyes in strange contrast to the people of the countryside, clad in leggings and a smock, and no shoes on his feet whatever the weather.

He had with him now, as always, a sack which he carried across one shoulder and which contained his fiddle and bow, the tools of his trade, and as often as not, a fat rabbit or silver salmon poached from the estates of some English lord. And with him too was his dog, Ruby, a creature as mongrel as he, blind in one eye, part collie, part terrier, unkempt, vicious, but the best dog in Ireland, I believe, for running down rabbits or hares.

"Top of the morning to you," said Tom when he was within hailing distance. "A great day it is with the west wind coming in over the sea and sweeping the country like the grace of the Blessed Mother." And with that he crossed himself, for he affected a certain piety knowing it was politic to do so.

"Good morning to you yourself," I replied, and then, picking up my spade, set once more to work. Tom, I suspected, had news. But he was never a man to part with it if any curiosity was shown. The best way to find out what he had on his mind was to go on with what you were doing. Then the news would boil and bubble inside of

2

him like water in a pot upon a fire, and he would out with it.

Tom seated himself on his sack (first removing his fiddle and bow) and looked around as nervous as a ferret at my cabin down in the hollow and out at the sea which lay beyond the cliffs a quarter of a mile away and then down at the pile of potatoes newly unearthed by myself that very morning.

"Ah," he said. " 'Tis the salvation of the people of the land, them spuds. I've often thought that when the Good Lord (and he crossed himself at the words) decided that there should be such a queer thing as a potato, he had the plight of the Irish people in mind."

"And I suppose," I replied, digging very heartily, "that when he invented the musket he was thinking of the plight of the English soldiery." For I was very hot against the English who had made it impossible at the time for an Irishman to be anything but a pauper in his own land.

Tom ignored my remark. He was in a mood to philosophize before giving me whatever news he had come with and would allow nothing to distract him. " 'Tis one of the wonders of the world," he said, "how everything precious that man may have or look for lies in the ground. Take gold, now. Where do they find it but buried in the bowels of the earth? 'Tis the same with silver and copper. The brightest rubies and the most

3

brilliant diamonds, and emeralds, as green as the
water in the caves at the bottom of the sea—all
of them come from the ground. Iron too and the
peat that we burn in our cabins, likewise the coal
that the English have by the thousand ton; stone
for houses and springs that are the start of great
rivers like the Shannon, all of them come of the
earth. Likewise, the potato."

At that he stopped for a while to search for a
bit of clay pipe which he had in the bottom of
his sack. He knew the contents of his sack so well
that in a matter of seconds he had his pipe, his
tinder box and his quid of tobacco. Another man
would have taken twenty minutes to find three
such small items in so large and untidy a space.

"The potato," said Tom, lighting his pipe with
great solicitude. "And what kind of a crop do you
think there's going to be, Kevin, me boy?"

Now I had been digging for some four hours,
and had lifted scarcely a sack of potatoes, most of
them undersized and many of them just shriveled
up little warts, as it were, at the bottom of the
plant. "If it goes on like this," I said, "it will be the
poorest crop since the famine."

"Ah," said Tom. He was silent for a while,
holding his bit of pipe between the three fingers
of his right hand from which he took his name.
"I've traveled far in the last two weeks," he said.
"Clear across Ireland from Dublin, working here
and there and playing a little and picking up the

news. When I started out the people were just beginning to harvest the early potato crop. And it's the same everywhere. In Louth and Cavan and West Meath and Longford and Roscommon and Galway it's all the same. The early potato crop is bad. Very bad."

My heart sank at those words. Potatoes were the sole food of the people of Ireland. They had nothing else to live by. If the potato crop failed, there would be nothing ahead but bitter hunger and perhaps starvation. "Tom," I said, "do you think there'll be a famine?"

He did not reply directly. Instead, he said, "When I was in Roscommon and Longford I saw clouds of swallows gathering on the trees ready to fly to Africa or wherever it is that they spend the winter. They're a month ahead of their time.

"Ruby has hardly raised a hare or a rabbit in fifty miles though the country should be thick with them.

"Do you know what I think? I think it's going to be one of the hardest winters that there's ever been in Ireland. The birds and the animals know these things before we do and get ready for them."

"Do you think there'll be a famine?" I persisted. I had grim memories of the great famine of 1846. It had taken my father, and six older brothers, and a sister, leaving only my mother and myself. The word famine sounded like a sentence of death to me.

5

"Tell me," said Tom. "What do the roots of the potatoes look like—the plants that failed?"

"They're covered with little warts," I replied.

"And the leaves themselves?"

"They've small brown holes in them. On some of the plants the leaves were almost withered away as if from drought."

"Then," said Tom, "I think there'll be a famine. I'd advise you to dig up every potato plant you have in the ground, whether it's ready for digging or not. For I tell you that as surely as I sit here that if you wait until December, you'll dig and find nothing but rottenness under the ground for your troubles."

He rose, whistled to his dog, put his tobacco, tinder box, and pipe in his sack and slung it upon his shoulders.

"Will you not stay the evening with us at the cabin?" I asked. "We'd be honored to have your company."

"Spoken like the nobility ye're descendent from," said Tom, "for it's well known that before the coming of the English, the O'Connors were kings of Connaught and indeed of all Ireland."

"They're not kings of their own potato patch now," I said. "But what we have we will gladly share with you." This was indeed true though my mother, remembering the former place our family had held, had taught me both to read and

6

write and instructed me to bear myself like a gentleman though born a pauper.

"I'd sooner be with you than in a palace," said Tom with great sincerity. "I'll go down to the cabin and pass the time of day with your mother. I've a little gift for her."

With that he left me, and I went on with my digging, very troubled in my mind at the thought of a potato famine. As I dug my anger rose at the condition which had reduced my mother and me to dependence for life on a quarter acre of ground on which to raise potatoes. That quarter acre of ground was rented from Mr. Tobias Henshaw, who rented it from Mr. James Colley, who rented it from Mr. Dan Heatherington, who was the agent of Lord Wedcomb, the aged Englishman who owned most of the land in Galway.

Each landlord raised the rent in subletting. I remember hearing from my father that Lord Wedcomb, through his agent Heatherington, received five shillings a year from our quarter acre. But Mr. Colley, the tenant who rented the land from Heatherington, had himself sublet it to Mr. Henshaw for ten shillings. And we leased it from Mr. Henshaw for one pound. We were lucky to get it. There were others who could have bid one pound five shillings for the land and put us out, though out of sympathy for my mother, none had done so yet.

You may wonder how I managed to raise the

pound with which to pay the rent for the land since at the time there was no employment in Ireland at which I or my fellow countrymen could earn money. I made it with fishing and taking the fish to Galway to sell. Out of this I could be sure of thirteen or fourteen shillings a year. The balance I earned by helping Mr. Forster, a farrier of Galway, shoe horses during the hunting season.

This year, with the rent due, I was four shillings short, but I had a plan by which to raise the money. Every September there was a fair held in Galway when a circus came to the town. One of the circus attractions was the strong man, who would pay four shillings to anyone who could wrestle with him for four minutes and not be thrown.

Most of our local boys and men tried their strength against the strong man, but he never parted with the four shillings to them. He was much too strong for any of them, even Dan Blainey, a blacksmith of Galway and a friend of mine. But I had watched the failures of others and so hoped to succeed, having concluded that the best strategy was to keep out of the strong man's grasp for the time required. To test strength against him was hopeless.

In a week I would have my chance to try. The money was vitally needed and I must succeed. No grace was ever allowed for rent payment. If the money was not handed over on the date due, we would be evicted.

I returned to our cabin that evening in bad spirits, full of hatred and resentment, all of it directed, as it usually was, against the English and Lord Wedcomb whose face no living man in Galway could ever recall having seen; for though his lordship owned the greater part of the land about, he had never once been to Ireland.

As I stood for a moment outside our cabin door, I heard Tom of the Three Fingers saying to my mother, "Never lose heart. Kevin may be the one to find the Foggy Dew."

They both fell silent as I entered.

CHAPTER TWO

———

To Enrich Our Dinner That Night Tom of the Three Fingers had brought a salmon taken out of one of Lord Wedcomb's streams. It was a fish of perhaps six pounds—"a mere sliver of a fish" as Tom himself put it. But we ate it all with the potatoes which normally formed our diet and had what might be called a banquet, the whole washed down with pepper water.

During the meal, Tom was full of talk picked up during his journeyings. He was a wonderful talker and seemed to attract the strangest adventures, or perhaps it was that he could make a tale out of the most commonplace of happenings. Thus he told us of the ghost horse of Derry, which every night was seen to run around the walls of the city, with four human skeletons on its back, the smallest no bigger than your hand and the biggest so huge that its boney feet trailed on the ground. The ghost horse, said Tom, appeared only when some terrible event was about to take place.

Again he recounted how there had been a terrible wind in Waterford which had driven the sea up through the city so that when the wind died and the waters subsided, there were several houses with ships upon their roofs. And he said that there had been a plague of grasshoppers in county Mayo so thick that several horses and cows had been suffocated by them. How true these stories were I have no way of judging, but in listening to Tom, nobody was concerned with the mere truth of his tales. It was the excitement of them and the fascinating details which he provided, all presented as sincerely as if he were talking to the Pope, that gave them their interest.

He never once touched upon the potato shortage, and I was grateful for this. If famine came, it would be bad enough, but I could see no sense in worrying my mother, now in her sixtieth year, about it in advance of the event.

My mind, however, kept going back to the sentence I had overheard before entering the hut —that maybe I would be the one who would find the Foggy Dew. I had heard vague references, when my father was alive, to the Foggy Dew, but had no clear concept of what was referred to. Since he died, I had never again heard the name until that night.

I determined then to find out what I could about this Foggy Dew and in a silence which followed one of Tom's stories, I put the question directly to my mother.

"I overheard you and Tom talking about the Foggy Dew before I came in the cabin," I said. "Tom said that maybe I would be the one to find it. What is the Foggy Dew?—for if I am to find it at all, I must certainly know what it is I am looking for."

"It's nothing but an old woman's tale," said my mother. "Just foolishness. Nothing to trouble your mind about." She passed a thin and heavily veined hand over her hair—a gesture which I knew from experience meant that she was upset.

Yet my curiosity was aroused. The very name intrigued me, and I would not be put off.

"I don't think you and Tom would have been talking so seriously about an old woman's tale, mother," I said. "I would like to know."

"I think the boy should be told," said Tom. "There's more truth to old legends and family stories than people are prepared to believe. I for one believe in the Foggy Dew as surely as I believe that it was one of Lord Wedcomb's salmon that we ate this very evening."

My mother gave a hopeless little shrug to indicate that she had been beaten in the argument and accepted the result. "It's a story which has brought bad luck and hardship to this boy's family for several centuries," she said to Tom. "I had hoped that in keeping him in ignorance of it, he might escape. But I see you are both against me, so go ahead."

"Bad luck it brought indeed," said Tom. "And sudden death and madness, they say, and many trials. And yet there is great happiness to be had for the man who again finds the Foggy Dew and that man may well be Kevin."

"Come," I said, full of impatience. "We've been beating around the bush long enough. Tell me the tale." But my heart was pounding as I spoke the words and my mouth seemed uncomfortable and dry.

"Well then," said Tom, looking deep into the fire as if it was in its burning heart that the whole story was written, "first as to what the Foggy Dew itself it. You've heard no doubt of precious stones like diamonds and rubies and emeralds and pearls and so on. But have you ever heard tell of an opal?"

"No," I replied.

"It's not to be wondered at," said Tom, "though there are a hundred different kinds of opals, maybe a thousand, and most of them not worth the trouble of stooping down to pick up.

"But there's one kind of opal so rare that it is worth a king's ransom. It is the black opal, the stone of midnight, as they call it. But it is a midnight in which may be seen all the colors of heaven, flaming reds, brilliant gold, silver, azure and emerald and every color known to man, as if a rainbow had been trapped in a black bowl. These colors move and change all the time. The

Foggy Dew is a black opal—a black opal as big as a walnut."

He paused then, to light his pipe, and took, it seemed to me, an eternity about it.

"Now," he said at length, "you know what the Foggy Dew is. But you do not know where it came from nor how it should affect you. And to tell you the truth, there is no man living who knows for certain where the Foggy Dew first came from.

"The story which I have heard most often about it is that it once belonged to Joseph of Arimathea, the rich Jew in whose sepulchre the body of Our Lord was laid after his crucifixion. But that hardly concerns my tale except to show that the stone is very old. It is certain that it was once owned by one of the kings of Hungary and the beauty of the stone is said to have driven him mad. From Hungary it was taken to France and from there to Spain where it became the property of the Spanish kings.

"Now you will remember perhaps that at one time the king of Spain sent a great fleet called the Armada against Queen Elizabeth of England. The fleet was put in charge of the Duke of Medina Sidonia and was so big, they say, that you could have walked dry shod from England to France across the decks of the Spanish vessels. Be that as it may, the duke brought with him the Foggy Dew, though advised against doing so. For the

14

Foggy Dew had already got an evil reputation, it being said that whoever would find it or hold it, must suffer terrible hardships.

"It is a matter of history that the Spanish fleet was utterly destroyed, and traveling around Scotland and then Ireland on the way back to Spain, the surviving vessels were subject to such storms as were never before seen at sea.

"Several of the Spanish galleons were thrown up on the coast, not a quarter of a mile from here. And among the poor wretches who survived the seas and rocks and gained the shore alive, was a Spaniard of noble birth. He was found by the servants of an ancestor of yours, Fergus O'Connor, who at the time was lord of all the lands around here. The man when he was found was lying on the top of Spaniard's Hill (it is from him that the hill takes its name). He was completely naked and his mind had gone from him. He lived for a year and could give little account of himself though by his manner it was plain that he had had a gentleman's upbringing. But the strangest circumstance of all was that when he was found, he had clenched in his fist, so hard that it had left a bruise on the palm of his hand, the Foggy Dew."

Tom of the Three Fingers fell quiet for a while to let the impact of this statement sink in. I recall that as he said "the Foggy Dew" there was a sudden whirl of wind around the cabin, and the smoke was blown back down the chimney so that

15

it spread for a minute or two like a white shroud before the fireplace. No doubt it was nothing but a natural coincidence. But my mother gave a start and crossed herself, and her face went very white.

"I wish you had never begun talking about the Foggy Dew," my mother said, a tremble in her voice. "Such talk will bring us no good. I had hoped to hear the last of it when the boy's father died."

"Ah 'twas nothing but a scurry of wind," said Tom. "The soul of the day going to the other side of the world and nothing more." Yet he too watched the smoke anxiously as it drifted back slowly up the chimney.

"Well," continued Tom. "I'll get on with the tale. The poor Spanish gentleman, as I've hinted, never recovered his full wits and so could give no account of how the stone had come into his possession. Fergus O'Connor hid him for the year that he lived in the big house that used to stand where this cabin is now. Elizabeth's soldiers scoured the countryside killing every Spaniard they could find, but they never found the man who had the Foggy Dew. And when he died, he gave the stone to Fergus.

"Up to then, the estates of the O'Connors, though diminished by years of warfare with the English and with other Irish chieftains, had been preserved. But when Fergus O'Connor gained possession of the Foggy Dew, the fortunes of the family changed.

"Fergus himself was found dead in a bog. He had two sons, Michael and Sean, and they both hated each other. Michael killed Sean and took over the family lands. But he himself was burned to death, and so it went on until two hundred years ago during the time of the Cromwell wars. At that time the chief of the O'Connors was Phelim—a big red-headed bear of a man, so sinful it was said that the grass withered wherever he put his foot down.

"I could tell you a thousand stories about Phelim O'Connor, but all of them would shame you. Murder was an amusement with him. He was a man who had no mercy in him. He had the blood of twenty men on his hands if he had the blood of one, but he was so feared and powerful that nobody could stand or rise against him. It's told that when a judge was sent out from Dublin especially to seize and try him, Phelim O'Connor and his crew of blackguards waylaid the judge and his escort, set up a court of their own, tried the judge, and Phelim hanged him himself, finding him guilty of cannibalism because the judge confessed to having breakfasted off pork that morning.

"Ah, he was a wicked man was Phelim O'Connor. None more wicked ever walked the face of the earth and it was common talk in his time,

I've heard say, that the Foggy Dew had driven him insane.

"But it was the Foggy Dew that put an end to him, for he and the stone disappeared the same night. Towards dusk one evening, according to the old tale, he rode alone to the top of the Spaniard's Hill. And while he was there, like a statue against the evening sky, a white mist came between him and the people in the house who were watching him. And when the mist cleared, horse, rider, and Foggy Dew had disappeared for good and all."

When Tom concluded his tale, my mind was so full of it that for a while I could think of nothing to say though a hundred questions pressed to be asked. It was strange that the least important should be the one that came to my tongue first.

"Why was the black opal called the Foggy Dew?" I asked.

"The name is part of the story of the stone," replied Tom quietly. "Whenever it has appeared, and whenever it has disappeared—and it disappeared many times though I haven't given you all the instances—there has always been a strange white mist just before the event."

"And why do you think I should be the one to find it—or would want to find it since it brought nothing but grief and hardship to those who owned it?" I said.

"Because," replied Tom, "another part of the

legend of the stone is that it shall be finally found by the seventh son of the seventh son. And you are the seventh boy in your family as your father was the seventh boy in his. And when the seventh son of the seventh son finds the Foggy Dew it will bring him all that he desires in the world.

"But," he concluded, "it will only be found after great hardship."

CHAPTER THREE

———

Tom Left the Following Morning, a tattered little man who, as he set off down the road, looked as though he might fall apart at any moment.

I had had a restless night of it, my mind being occupied even in my sleep with his tale of the Foggy Dew, interspersed with distorted snatches of the other stories Tom had told. One particular dream was so vivid that it lingered with me through the day. It was of a great mass of horses appearing out of a mist and ridden by skeleton riders. They thundered past me, the wind whistling through their bones, and on the head of each horse, set into the front of the skull between the eyes, was a gleaming jewel.

I went some part of the way with Tom, for I had a question or two more to ask him about the Foggy Dew, in particular whether he thought the stone might be found somewhere in the neighborhood of Spaniard's Hill. I should explain that this was not an ordinary grass- or gorse-covered hill, but a rocky place, full of boulders and outcrops, with immediately at the foot of it on the west side, sheer cliffs plunging down into the Atlantic.

Tom, however, was oddly uncommunicative. He did not seem to want to discuss the black opal any further. He contented himself by saying that it was unlikely that I would find the stone, if indeed I ever did, by searching for it.

"If the legend of the seventh son of the seventh son is true," he said, "the stone will find you. You will have hardship and trials of many kinds. And then, after the appearance of the white mist, you will find the stone. But," he added, though not with much conviction, "perhaps your mother is right and it is all nothing but an old wives' tale."

Before we parted, he being bound for the city of Galway eight miles distant, he said, "If ever the occasion should arise that you're in need of a friend and have no place to turn, get yourself to the 'Whistling Goat' on Quay Street, Dublin, and inquire for me there. As you know I spend my time from spring through autumn traveling around the countryside. But the 'Whistling Goat' is my headquarters during the winter months when the cold is on the land like the lid on a coffin."

With that he went, his dog Ruby at his heels, and I returned to my work digging potatoes.

The Saturday following Tom's visit was the day of the fair and circus in Galway. It was the day when, if I proved agile enough on my feet, I

21

might hope to win four shillings from the strong man with which to pay part of the rent for our holding. My mother could not accompany me to town. It was, as I have said, eight miles distant, and we had no transportation but our own feet. At her age the journey would be too much for her. I was glad she could not come for she knew nothing of my plans for raising the money and might have tried to prevent me carrying them out.

"I'll bring back some bright thing for you, mother," I told her as I left, "and still have money to pay the rent."

Galway was teeming with people when I arrived, and they were divided sharply into two classes—the poor and the rich; tenants and landlords. We of the tenantry were easy to distinguish by our clothing of which not an item was new and all of it the same dingy brown or gray. Yet there was a certain spirit among the tenantry, cracking jokes and greeting each other with whoops of delight and extravagant inquiries about health, and great solicitude if any kind of sickness was reported. As for the landlords and their agents, they were a people apart, riding good horses, well dressed, affecting hardly to notice the poorer sort, and thinking nothing to urging their steeds through a crowd of them as if they were not there.

There were a number of black looks and curses

sent after them, but to these they paid no attention.

Galway in those times was a walled city and the market was held in the center of the town, though the circus and fair was outside the walls. I stopped first at Mr. Forster, the farrier. He had a shilling for me for some work I had done for him a month ago. As usual he gave it as if it were charity and charity which he could ill afford. But that was just the manner of the man. He had spent his life pinching at pence to keep his business going, and it hurt him to the heart to part with a coin.

"Will you be wanting me to help you during the week, Mr. Forster?" I asked.

"You can meet me at the Wedcomb stables on Wednesday," he said. "There are two horses to be physicked and one to be shod. Sixpence is the price to you, if you do a good day's work."

"Horses at Wedcomb's stables?" I cried. "Why, there haven't been any horses kept at the stables for as long as I can remember." This was true, for the Earl of Wedcomb never lived in Ireland, and the stables were unoccupied though kept up by his agent.

"Well, there are some there now," said Mr. Forster. "Get along with you. I'll see you on Wednesday." With that I had to be satisfied. I had one or two friends to look up, among them Dan Blainey, the blacksmith, and I went with Dan out to the fair and circus outside the walls where we were to try our skill and strength against the strong man in the middle of the afternoon.

If Dan had one peculiarity by which he might be readily described it was his habit of whistling. He was a small fellow for a blacksmith, with reddish hair which exactly matched the color of the freckles spattered all over his face and forearms. Whatever he was doing, with the possible exception of eating his food and sleeping, he whistled. I believe he got this whistling habit when he was a boy watching his father at work in the smithy. Hostlers, farriers and blacksmiths have a habit of whistling when handling horses to quieten their nerves and Dan, watching his father at work, had learned to imitate him and now whistled all the time.

We went together to the fairground, Dan whistling tonelessly away and I busy with my thoughts of the coming encounter with the strong man. I had to stay in the ring with him for four minutes or lose our cottage and land. Now that the time for the encounter was near, I felt increasingly nervous.

The place where the strong man put on his display was in a large area before the animal cages. He had a roped platform of planks erected, perhaps four feet from the ground so that all could get a good view, and before he issued his challenge, it was his custom to give a demonstration of his strength.

24

This demonstration quelled many a prospective challenger, and was doubtless designed for that purpose.

"Has any of my friends around here got a good stout horseshoe?" the strong man, whose name was Mordor, would ask, and a dozen horseshoes would be offered him, for people brought them along especially for this demonstration.

He would take one, hold it up and show it to all around, and then taking it by the ends, his huge arm muscles bulging and his face growing a deep red, he would straighten the horseshoe out with his bare hands. The silence while he did this was almost as dramatic as the demonstration itself. I would catch myself holding my breath, the blood pounding in my ears, while Mordor forced the horseshoe into a straight line.

Dan and I were late in arriving this particular day. The crowd was almost impenetrable around Mordor's platform, and he had just concluded his horseshoe performance as we thrust our way through the mob.

"Now," he said, "I come to a part of my performance which astounded the Tsar of all the Russias and so impressed him that he presented me with the Ring of St. Stanislaus. Martha, show the good people the ring."

Nobody knew whether Martha was Mordor's wife or mother. She was the one who told fortunes when Mordor was not giving his demonstration.

She had a wrinkled brown face, strong white teeth, and always wore a short black velvet jacket and a full length skirt of bright green silk. She held up now a piece of scarlet satin on which there was a ring which might have been of gold or brass from all I could see of it.

This was displayed to the crowd who murmured in awe. I, myself, was not too impressed for the ring looked like the mate to the one which Martha had in her right ear.

With a great deal of elaboration Mordor now lay down on the platform. Three male assistants picked up a blacksmith's anvil and placed it upon his chest whereupon he made grimaces of great pain and endurance. Then one of the assistants took a six-pound sledge and while we all held our breath struck the anvil a heavy blow with it. I believe everyone present, myself included, groaned in agony as the huge hammer came down upon the anvil; everyone, that is, but Mordor, who merely closed his eyes and stiffened the muscles of his great chest.

Altogether he took six blows with the sledge and what was the most extraordinary thing about it was that there was not a single mark upon his chest where the weight of the anvil had lain. So it was plain that his very skin was as strong as the muscles that rolled and twisted behind it.

There were still two or three more feats of strength to be performed by Mordor before the issuing of his challenge—the bursting of a one-inch chain with his hands, the bending of iron spikes between the fingers of one hand, and finally biting a rod of iron in two with his teeth.

When all this had been done, and the whole crowd thoroughly quelled, the strong man stepped to the center of the ring.

"My friends and neighbors, good people all," he said, "it is my custom each year at this place, to challenge anyone who wishes to a test of strength against me. The terms of the challenge are these. The challenger is to receive one shilling a minute—think of that now—a day's pay for a minute's work, for every minute he can remain in this ring with me. But if he is thrown out in less than four minutes, he will receive nothing.

"Now who is there who would like to try his strength or skill against Mordor the Mighty?"

Daniel stopped whistling long enough to say that he would. He was quickly shoved into the ring, whistling again, and having stripped off his shirt and coat stood ready for Mordor. Clothed Daniel did not look like a big man. Next to Mordor, he seemed undersized. Yet he was ruggedly muscled, and if he had any wit to use his muscles, might have had a chance against the giant.

As it was, Daniel had only one method of fighting and that was to come to grips with his opponent. As Mordor came towards him, Daniel closed with the giant. And in a minute he was pinned quite helpless in the huge arms, and a second later, hurled out of the ring, to fall into the crowd amidst a great deal of laughter.

"Thirty-five seconds," said one of Mordor's assistants. "Is there anyone else?"

"Yes," I cried and pushed my way forward to the platform.

CHAPTER FOUR

IT SEEMED TO ME as I climbed unsteadily through the ropes to confront Mordor that time stopped and the emotions of a lifetime were crowded into a few seconds.

I recall as I bent my head to get under the rope that I saw in detail the faces of the people in the crowd looking up at me. It was as if I had an hour instead of merely a fraction of a second in which to study them. I remember one man with his mouth half open and the sun gleaming on his yellow teeth. And another who had a piece of straw in the corner of his mouth which waved solemnly up and down as he chewed the end of it. I saw the face of a boy, the eyes bright with excitement. And as I got into the ring and straightened up, I caught a glimpse of a youth on a horse forcing his way through the crowd to the edge of the platform.

There are some people who at first glimpse announce themselves as enemies, and that was my immediate reaction on catching sight of this youth. But I had not time to dwell on my feeling for him, for Mordor's assistants were already helping me out of my jacket and shirt and a silence went over the crowd like a sea enveloping it.

Standing in the crowd, separated from Mordor by perhaps thirty feet, I had no true idea of his huge size. Now that I was but four or five feet from him I could see that giant was an inadequate word for him. He was a monster. His head was of a size more fitted to a large animal than a man. It sat upon his shoulders almost without the intervention of a neck. And his shoulders were solid pads of muscle so that I no longer wondered that he could support the weight of an anvil on his barrel chest with ease.

"Time," cried Mordor's assistant and struck a piece of steel bar as a bell. Mordor came at me like an ape, shuffling flatfooted across the platform. The great trick, I knew, was not to get caught in a corner, and I backed away towards the center of one of the ropes. Mordor shuffled closer towards me, and using the rope at my back as a spring, I hurtled under his outstretched arms and into the center of the ring again. Mordor turned with a grunt to follow me. Of his strength, nobody could be in any doubt. But he moved slowly, and after my first evasion, I got a measure of confidence, and managed to avoid him for perhaps a minute with ease.

During the next minute, following the same tactics, the crowd grew angry at the lack of action.

They shouted at me to come to grips, not to keep running away, to fight like a man! But it was not they who were in need of the four shillings, but I. And it was not they who were in the ring either. Then someone threw a clod of earth and it hit me in the back. This brought shouts of laughter and encouragement to throw others. Then a voice—a very affected English voice—cut through the hubbub.

"Quiet," it said. "The man is a coward, it is plain to be seen. Let him give a public exhibition of his cowardice and let us be content with that. What is one to expect of cowards but continual running away?"

I turned to see who was speaking, my gorge rising. The speaker was the same youth on horseback whom I had glimpsed as I climbed into the ring. He was about my age, but extremely handsome, his head crowned by curly golden hair. I had never seen him before.

This fleeting distraction took but a second. But it was a second which cost me dear. Mordor was not distracted either by the clods thrown by the crowd nor the jeers directed at me. He grabbed at me and I was too late to evade him. I was lifted up as if I weighed no more than a straw, and flung from the ring, falling among my mockers. All my hopes of raising the four shillings to pay the rent due on our ground were now gone. I received a good buffeting from the crowd before

31

I managed to get out of it, and had to run pelted by clods and filth. These were men from Galway who did not know me, and they were determined to have their sport at my expense. When finally I eluded them, it was to be further humiliated by the young dandy on horseback. He rode up to me where I stood, still naked to the waist, for my shirt and coat were in the ring, and reining in his horse said in his contemptuous voice, "You have had your deserts, you craven. What have you to say for yourself?"

"Only this," I said, panting between anger and mortification, "that you have cost me four shillings I badly need. And if you will get off that horse, I'll show you who is the coward."

"Confounded insolence," said the rider. His handsome face went white and he struck at me with his riding crop, and then clapping spurs to his horse, galloped off.

Dan had by now found me.

"Who is that man?" I asked him.

"Never seen him before," replied Dan. "One of the gentry in for the fair, I suppose. We should be thankful for horses. If there were no such beasts, people like him would ride human beings. Here, put on your coat and shirt. I've brought them with me or you'd have lost them."

Dan did his best to cheer me up, but I could not be consoled. I had failed to get the four shillings, and there was but three days left in which to obtain it, for it was due the following Tuesday.

"Don't let it disturb you," Dan said. "Half the tenantry cannot pay their rents. You will not be thrown out. Ask for a month more and you will have time to raise the money."

But this did not comfort me. We had been warned several times by Mr. Henshaw that if we were as much as a day late we would be evicted. I went home bitterly depressed, and without buying the present for my mother which I had promised her. The shilling I had from Mr. Forster would be badly needed and could not be spent on trifles.

Tuesday, Mr. Henshaw was round for his rent. I gave him the shilling, said I had not got the balance, but if he would give me a few weeks, I believed I would be able to raise it for him. His face hardened immediately.

"I can give you until tomorrow night," he said. "Not an hour more."

"But we have always paid in the past," I said. "Surely you can give me a little time."

"I can give you until tomorrow night," he repeated. "I will be here at sunset and if you have not the money, you must get out."

"Mr. Henshaw," I pleaded, "you have dealt with my father and myself for many years. You know we have always paid. We've never been behindhand. One day is not enough."

"Things have changed," said Mr. Henshaw. "If

33

it were in my hands, I'd give you a week or a month. But the new Lord Wedcomb wants his rents in on the day appointed. And I must have the money."

"The new Lord Wedcomb?" I asked.

"The same," said Henshaw. "Hadn't you heard that the old lord died in London and his son is out here? He's dead set against the tenantry and seeking an excuse to get rid of them. His orders are that if their rents are not paid on time, the tenants are to be evicted that very day."

This was terrible news. Our cabin was no great place. It was built of sods with reinforcement of stone at the corners. The floor was of earth and the whole place little more than a shelter against the weather. Yet it was our home—our only home. To be evicted from it, penniless, without right of appeal (for the lord was the sole authority on what was done with his lands) was tantamount to a sentence of death. I had known of other evictions, and the tenants evicted had just disappeared, traveling the roads, joining the hordes of beggars without a place to go and dependent for their food upon charity.

When Mr. Henshaw had gone, I determined to go to Mr. Colley, from whom Mr. Henshaw rented the land, and if necessary to Mr. Heatherington, Lord Wedcomb's agent. But the journey was useless. Mr. Colley dismissed me curtly with the statement that the matter was no concern of his. He did not rent the land directly to us but to Mr. Henshaw and must have his money from Mr. Henshaw. As for Mr. Heatherington, although it was a four mile walk to his house, he had not even the grace to speak to me.

My sole remaining hope then, was a slim one. It was that the following day, Wednesday, I might be able to persuade Mr. Forster while working at the stables as arranged, to give me an advance of money against future employment with him. I told him the story as soon as we met, but far from being sympathetic, he flew into a great rage, complained that my work had always been poor (which I knew to be untrue), that he was not in the business of lending money, and that he had made it a rule all his life never to interfere in the financial affairs of others.

And so my last resource had gone and I became desperate. Not counting the sixpence which I was to receive for that day's work from Mr. Forster, I had to get half a crown—two shillings and sixpence—by dusk if I was to retain the small cabin and plot of land from which we obtained our livelihood. The sum was ridiculously small. Yet it might as well have been a thousand times the size for all my ability to raise it. There was no method by which I might earn it. There was no employment for me and no one who would lend it. I had nothing I could sell and no one to turn to. The only man who could with a word help me was Lord Wedcomb himself and he was as inaccessible to me as the Queen of England.

Desperation breeds action, quite often action so unreasonable as to border on the insane. After Mr. Forster had refused me a loan, or rather an advance against future work, my mind was in a whirl of fears and anxieties and I was close to a kind of mental panic. Out of this came one drive or urge which could not be denied. I must go myself to Lord Wedcomb, wherever he was to be found, and put my case to him.

That he was divided from my sort by layers of servants of all degrees, starting with the gate-keeper, all of whom would be intent, as their sacred duty, on keeping me from his lordship's presence, did not deter me. I let go of the halter of the horse which Mr. Forster was doctoring and without a word of explanation, strode from the stables in the direction of Wedcomb House.

CHAPTER FIVE

It Is Probable That I might never have managed to see Lord Wedcomb, because his household servants would have kept me from him, except for the coincidence that he was on his way to the stables as I set out to go to him.

As it was, I was walking along the graveled path that led to the manor between lawns as neat as the cloth on a billiard table, when he came towards me on a fine horse, accompanied by a young lady who, I later discovered, was his sister, Lady Barbara. I recognized him immediately and my heart fell. He was the same youth who had taunted me during my bout with Mordor and had gone out of his way to humiliate me after I had lost that fight.

He reined in when he caught sight of me, and called out in a sharp imperious voice, "What are you doing on my grounds?"

"I am looking for Lord Wedcomb," I replied.

"Well," he said, staring down at me so that I became acutely conscious of the poverty of my clothing, of my soiled hands and face and my unkempt hair, "what do you want of me?"

"My Lord," I said as humble as my feelings would allow, "I am one of the tenants on your land. My mother and I are to be evicted unless we can raise two shilling and sixpence to pay our rent by this evening. I came to ask that you would intercede on our behalf."

He looked at me for several seconds in utter astonishment. The astonishment was quite genuine. It shocked the habitual expression of disdain from his face.

"Intercede on your behalf?" he repeated. "In Heaven's name, did you ever hear of such an astonishing request? Why should I intercede on your behalf? I come over from England on the death of my father to find my estates swarming with rats and vermin like yourself, my lands covered with little hovels in which you live. And then you ask me to help you continue to hold on to this little hovel.

"I will tell you something that you can tell to your fellows. Inside of six months I will have cleared you all off of my lands—every man, woman and child of you, and use the ground to raise some decent clean kind of beast, like cattle or horses.

"Take back that message to your fellows. And get out of my way." With that he spurred his horse forward so suddenly as to nearly knock me down, and galloped away, his sister with him, leaving me trembling with rage and mortification.

I did not bother to return to the stables to Mr. Forster. I could not have worked, so great was the agitation of my mind. Instead I went over to Galway, intending to see Dan. I knew he had little or no money. His blacksmith work brought him in just enough to buy his iron and keep him alive. Yet he might have some advice to offer, or might be able through friends to raise the small amount of two shillings and sixpence, which I must have by that evening.

During the long walk my mind quietened down a little. I recalled that Lord Wedcomb had said he intended to clear all his tenants off his land. That meant mass eviction on the Wedcomb estates—an eviction very easy to achieve since none of the tenants had any legal hold on the land. Leases were denied them. The very cabins which they built with their own hands were, under the law, the property of Lord Wedcomb. He could pull them down by sending crowbar gangs to wreck them. And other cabins had been pulled down on other estates by crowbar gangs, pulled down although some of the occupants were sick and had to be moved out into the open.

Thinking of this on my way to Galway, with the autumn sun gilding the Atlantic to my right, and the curlews giving their lonesome cry and flagging slowly over the fields, it came to me that I was not alone. All the tenants on the Wedcomb estates would be in the same position as I in six months time. What if we refused to leave our cabins? What if, when anyone was to be evicted, all the other tenants came to his cabin and drove the wrecking crews away? We were more numerous than the landlords and their agents and their wrecking crews. We could enforce our will on them and would be no longer at the mercy of landlord and landlord's agents.

My heart beat faster as this plan evolved in my mind, and I was full of excitement when I found Dan at work in his shop and told him of it.

He whistled as was his custom all through my explanation, seated astride his anvil and staring moodily into his smoldering forge.

"They have the law on their side," he said. "They'd call out the militia and fire on you and that would be the end of your plan."

"Well," I said, "let them call out the militia on us. All we have to lose is our lives. And we are likely to lose them anyway by hunger if we are driven off our lands."

"You can try," said Dan. "But I don't think you'll get much support. See how many neighbors you can get to your cabin this evening, for I haven't a doubt that his lordship will send a crowbar crew over with Mr. Henshaw in case you haven't got the money."

There were twenty cabins within a quarter-mile radius of our own, and though I visited every one of them, it is shameful to say that only

40

half a dozen men would agree to help me. I have never known such a pack of cowards and felt that Lord Wedcomb's description of his tenants as rats was warranted. To be sure they sympathized. To be sure they said that it was an unchristian act to turn us out for lack of two shillings and six-pence rent. To be sure their faces went white when I told them of Lord Wedcomb's threat to clear his land of the tenantry in six months time and they railed against him. But when it came to the point of making a stand, and that right now, their hearts failed them.

They still had their cabins and their land. They had paid their rents or had hope of paying them. Nothing had been said to them about eviction directly by the landlord's agents. They were sorry for me and sorry for my mother. But they clung to the hope that the fate which loomed before us, they might somehow avoid. They were desper-ately anxious not to do anything that would anger Lord Wedcomb, and at several of the cabins I was made something less than welcome when I began to unfold my plan.

Of the half dozen who joined me, one was a man in his sixties, Tim O'Phelan. He had a long white beard and a face as full of folds of skin as a bloodhound's. In his youth he must have been a big fine figure of a man. His old shoulders still had the shadow of strength on them, and when he spoke it was in a deep voice, increasing his likeness to a biblical prophet.

"Kevin O'Connor," he said, "your family and mine have fought side by side through many years. Your people were kings in these parts and mine servant to no man. I'll come with you. I'm the last of my line for the famine of forty-six took them all but me. And you are the last of yours. I wouldn't leave you now. For the old times."

"Thank you," I said simply, for I could find no more adequate words.

"Wait a minute until I get Liberty," he said. We were talking in his cabin. He lived alone on a little plot. He took a rough bench and placed it in one corner of the cabin and climbed on it. He thrust a lean arm into a recess atop the cabin wall and pulled out a pike. I had heard of pikes many a time but this was the first one I'd seen. The shaft, of oak, was about six feet long; the head, like a huge butcher's knife, slightly curved backwards. The metal of the head and the handle of the shaft shone, so it was plain that Tim O'Phelan spent a great deal of time polishing "Liberty" and kept the pike in a good condition.

"A dozen at least of the English have died from arguing with 'Liberty,'" said Tim. "In Fitzgerald's rising," he added, "at the storming of Newry, we charged the redcoats with the pike. They stood like a wall, firing at us with their muskets. We stopped for a while, frightened. Then Barry

Burke, who was next to me, let out a wild whoop and the others took it up and so we came on and the redcoats broke and ran. They'd had all the discipline in the world at standing still, but they had no practice whatever in running. So we cut them down by the score. A pike will leave a terrible wound in a man, I tell you. Worse than a musket ball. There was blood half way up the shaft and I had to stop in the middle of the slaughter to wipe it clean for it was too slippery to hold.

"Ah, they were great days. We *fought* then! Now we just bow down and say, 'Good day, my Lord.' 'Good day, Mr. Rent Collector and I hope ye are very well.' We're the greatest 'Good day' people in the world. Things have changed. There's no spirit left in the country."

When he had finished, old Tim gave a savage thrust with the pike into the sod wall of his cabin, so that the head of the weapon was buried deep. "A terrible wound a pike leaves," he said, pulling it out. "I heard an English captain say once that he would sooner stand up to French artillery at point-blank range than a charge of Irish pikemen."

I did not know quite what to say. It was not my intention to stimulate any violence—but just to have a sufficient force of neighbors with me to dissuade the crowbar gang from pulling down our cabin. Bloodshed was a different matter. I didn't want any of that.

43

"Tim," I said, "I'll be glad of your presence. But I think it would be better to leave your pike behind. We don't want bloodshed. And in any case, if you're seen with the pike you can be arrested for carrying arms."

"Let your mind rest easy," said Tim. "I'm a decent law-abiding man and wouldn't walk around carrying arms for all the world." With that he whipped the head off his pike, put it in a piece of cloth and tied it around his waist so that it was hidden by his coat. "Now," he said holding out the shaft, "they can't quarrel with an old man carrying a staff to lean on and help him over the rough places in the road."

Of the other five who joined, two were men who had already been told that by the end of the week, unless they raised a few shillings apiece, they were to be evicted. They came then to my aid, with a promise that I would come to help them. Three others were relatives of these, and there were a few women and their children. We formed a ragged little group, not quite sure of what we were up against, nor of what tactics we would adopt, nor of how far we would carry our resistance. Indeed, I can say that we were sure of only one thing. And that was that we were going to try to stop the first eviction of a tenant from the lands of the new Lord Wedcomb.

As we walked, with the sun sinking rapidly and a cold wind coming from the Atlantic, old Tim struck up a bit of a tune. It was the "Wearing of the Green," and we sang the verses all the way through. We felt excited and bold and ready for any adventure and I felt my blood tingling with a kind of wild anticipation as we topped Spaniard's Hill and came down the other side to the fold in the hills where our cabin lay.

CHAPTER SIX

———

WHEN WE GOT CLOSE TO OUR CABIN, Dan came running up the hill to meet me. I believe it was the first time in my life that I'd seen him run, for he was a man of slow movement both mental and physical, his actions having all the solidity of the iron which he worked.

"Kevin," he said, "you'd better tell them to go back. The story is around that you're leading a body of armed men here and the militia have been sent for. They're on their way from Galway now. I warned you that they'd call out the militia."

All who were with me heard Dan say this and looked at me awaiting my reply. "We carry no arms," I said. "And there is no law to stop us being here."

"It would be better," said Dan, "if they all went away. I've taken your mother into Galway to my lodging, in case of trouble. But you know these militia. They're just play-soldiers. They've no discipline and are eager for a chance to shoot at anything and prove themselves heroes."

I turned to the little group around me. "You've

heard the news," I said bitterly. "If any of you want to leave, I won't think hard of you."

"I'm staying for one," said old Tim. "I don't give a fig for militia. I've chased a score of them in my time if I've chased one. Redcoats are something different, but militia, pshaw." And he spat on the ground as if to blot out all the militia in Ireland.

"I don't know what I'm here for," one of the men said, looking as foolish and lost as a child.

"To stop my mother and me being evicted and our cabin being pulled down. It may be your turn next," I replied.

"But I hadn't bargained for the militia," the man said.

"Nor I," replied another.

"I'm a peace-loving man and don't like bloodshed," said a third.

"I've my wife and children at home waiting in tears this very moment," said a fourth. And so it went on. They had not the courage to say plainly that they were afraid and were going back. They stood there making excuses for themselves, trying to put as good a light on their fears as they could, and yet not one could bring himself to be the first to move off.

It was one of the women who finally put some heart into them. "Shame upon you all for a pack of cowards!" she cried. "Would you let a young boy and his mother be robbed of their home and

47

their livelihood and stand there making excuses for not doing anything to help them?

"Well, run then, the whole bunch of you! What kind of men are you that are afraid of the shadow of the militia even before the militia themselves have come? Go home to your sons and teach them to be cowards like yourselves and sorrow on the day for Ireland for there are no true men left in the land."

"Will you hold yer tongue, woman," said one of the men sharply. "You've a voice would drive a corpse from its coffin."

"Nobody said anything about running away," said another. "It's a proper thing to debate the odds before there's any fighting."

"I've never run away from anything in me life," said a third.

"Well then," said the woman, all the acid out of her now, and her voice as sweet as honey, "if you want to run, you'd better start, for here come the militia now."

It was true. They came in a tattered array, a body of perhaps twenty led by a very big man on a very small pony. We gaped at them and my heart sank. Against that number there was nothing we could do. As these men came nearer I could see that what I had taken for muskets and fowling pieces carried by some of them were not guns at all but crowbars. Mr. Henshaw was with them, and when the man on the pony had come up to us, he reached in the pocket of his cloak and pulled out a roll of paper.

"In accordance with the laws of the realm, passed for the advancement of the public good and the protection of property," he said, "I am now going to read the Riot Act. If at the end of the reading of this act, this present unruly and riotous company, gathered to disturb the Queen's peace, has not dispersed, I will order the militia to fire one round over their heads. If they do not then disperse, I will call upon the militia to fire into them."

He fumbled in another pocket and took out a pair of spectacles which he placed with much ceremony on his nose. Unfortunately for him, while he was doing this, his pony shifted her footing and his scroll of paper, which I presumed contained the wording of the Riot Act, fell to the ground.

Tim picked it up immediately, but before handing it back to its owner, glanced over it.

"This isn't the Riot Act," he said. "It's a blank piece of paper—"

"Give that to me," said the horseman and snatched it away from old Tim.

"Now," he continued, "I will start the reading of this act and you remain here at your peril."

"But you haven't got the Riot Act with you," said Tim.

"That is of no consequence," said the man. "I know it by heart."

Holding the blank piece of paper before him, he recited as follows, "Our Sovereign Lady the Queen chargeth and commandeth all persons being assembled to disperse themselves, and peaceably to depart to their habitations or to their lawful business, upon the pains contained in the act made in the first year of King George for preventing tumultuous and riotous assemblies. God Save the Queen."

All this was delivered in a mechanical tone and when he had concluded, the magistrate, for such he was, said, "Now, off with you. If you remain,

"You may have ten minutes to get them out,"

All the men went, except old Tim. The women followed with the exception of the one who had railed at the men for cowardice. She stood to one side watching but saying nothing.

Mr. Henshaw now came forward, deeming it safe. "Do you have the rent due to me?" he asked.

"No," I replied. "Can't you give me a little more time?"

"The orders coming to me from Lord Wedcomb are that if the rent is not paid, the cabin is to be pulled down," he said.

"What about our furniture and pots inside?" I asked.

you must suffer the lawful consequences."

said Mr. Henshaw, producing a watch. "Ten minutes and no more."

I went into the cabin with old Tim who helped me carry my truckle bed and my mother's to the side of the road. We carried out several sacks of potatoes too, and the few pots which we used for cooking. Nobody else offered to help with this work and when it was done, Mr. Henshaw nodded to the militia men. These advanced on the cabin with their crowbars which they plunged into the walls, ripping out the turf and stones of which the walls were made. They might as well have plunged them into my heart, for the pain was as bad.

When a house which has sheltered people for many years is being wrecked it is like murder. The cabin groaned at the wounds which were being made in its sides. It seemed to cry for help as the stones which formed the corners of the walls were prized out and tumbled to the ground. I sat on my bed by the side of the road, my head in my hands for I could not bear to watch.

When they were halfway through, Lord Wedcomb arrived on his horse and accompanied by his sister, Lady Barbara.

"Ah," he cried in his disdainful voice, "I see we have made a start on the extermination of the hovels of these wretches." Everybody, including the men with the crowbars stopped to bow to him and say, "Good evening, my Lord." He got down from his horse, and passing directly before me,

51

but without paying me the slightest attention, walked towards the half-demolished cabin.

"A sty," he pronounced. "A sty in which I would not keep my pigs," and he kicked at some of the turf which had been pulled from the walls. This was more than I could bear. I was on him before anyone could stop me, and seizing him by the shoulder spun him around to face me.

"Take this, then, from a pig," I cried, and struck him so hard that he staggered back, stumbled over some of the turf and fell sprawling on his back. For a second nobody moved. All were stunned by the swiftness of my attack. Then I heard Tim cry out and saw him charge at the militia. He had put the head on his pike, Liberty, and the cry he let out was high-pitched and terrible. The militia scattered before him, and there was the heavy roar of a musket and the higher pitched crack of a pistol and I saw old Tim go down in a crumpled heap to the ground.

Then Lady Barbara came up to me on her horse. She slid swiftly from it, saying, "Get on my horse and ride. Ride! They will kill you."

All this happened at once. It could not have been more than a few seconds from the time I knocked Lord Wedcomb down to the time I found myself astride Lady Barbara's horse, galloping away in the direction of Spaniard's Hill. I took one quick look behind me, and saw there was no pursuit. On foot the militia could not hope to catch me. And Lord Wedcomb did not have the inclination or perhaps the courage to attempt the pursuit alone.

But I knew that I would be hunted down. In one day my life had changed so that now I was an outlaw wanted, without a doubt, for the crimes of inciting to riot and attacking a nobleman.

I drove my bare heels hard at the sides of the horse and it plunged up the rocky slopes of Spaniard's Hill. The sun had now set and as I reached the crest, a white mist came in from over the sea, enveloping me and the horse.

CHAPTER SEVEN

AT THE TOP OF SPANIARD'S HILL, the mist now so thick around me that I could scarcely see the ground below the horse's hooves, I reined in to consider what to do next. This mist filled me with deep fear and foreboding, for I recalled immediately the story of that ancestor of mine who had disappeared with the Foggy Dew in just such a mist as this.

I trembled with fright and anxiety and did not know where to turn or what to do next. I knew that the hue and cry would soon be raised—that awful instrument whereby a man is run down like a hare, with all his neighbors forced to join in the chase. Bloodhounds would be used. And there was nowhere I could go, for no man dared offer me shelter. The houses of those who were known to be my friends would be watched, and I would put them in great peril were I to approach any of them.

Plainly I must get out of this part of Ireland, and my horse was at one and the same time an aid and a peril to me. It would be expected that I would be riding so on that score I would be wiser to get rid of the horse. Yet mounted I could go much further than afoot, and in hot pursuit would have more chance of getting away.

While I was thinking all this over, I heard a slight sound behind me. It was nothing more than the noise a small stone would make rolling over the ground. But in the deep silence of the mist it startled me, and a second later the horse whinnied and I believed all lost. Then from out of the mist came a woman's voice.

"Are you there, Kevin O'Connor?" she said.

"Who is it?" I asked.

"A friend," was the answer. "Stay where you are." Out of a mist a figure came towards me, spectre-like and distorted by the whiteness around. She came within a few feet of the horse.

"Who are you and what are you doing here?" I asked.

She ignored the question. "Dismount and follow me," she said. "Bring the horse with you and make as little noise as you can. The militia are surrounding the bottom of the hill, and when they're all in place, they'll close in on you. Come."

She led the way carefully down the steeper side of the hill which, as I have said, plunged in a precipice into the Atlantic. The horse pulled back on its bridle, unwilling to trust itself to the slope in the mist and darkness. When we had gone perhaps twenty yards, the woman stopped beside a big boulder.

"From here it gets dangerous," she said. "I'm

troubled about the horse. You had better ride him. It will give him confidence." The way now led past the boulder, and I sensed from the coldness of the air on my left side and the freshness of the breeze which carried billows of mist with it, that we were on a narrow track directly over the ocean. The woman went forward confidently enough. But the track was no more than a foot wide and the horse trembled beneath me. At the time I wondered why she wanted to bring the horse down here at all.

How long we descended by this goat path along the precipice I do not know. It seemed like several hours to me, but perhaps was for little more than fifteen or twenty minutes. All the time I was haunted by the fear of pursuit. Finally we stopped.

"This is the place," the woman said. "It is a cave. You will have to get down. It is very dark. Take my hand and follow me." Dark was hardly the word for it. The blackness had a sort of solidity to it which seemed to press upon me. I found myself crouching and tensed, expecting at any moment to strike my head upon a boulder, or step off of some ledge and go hurtling down. The air seemed heavy with moisture and there was a continual sound of dripping water which was most melancholy to hear.

After a while the woman let go of my hand, I heard her striking a flint and a steel and soon she had lit a candle lantern which she had brought with her and I was able to look around.

We were in a large cave whose walls were festooned with ugly moss which dripped constantly. The floor was of gravel, and water from the dripping moss flowed over this to join a small stream which entered one side of the cave and left through a crevice on the other side.

I turned to look at the woman who had come so unexpectedly to my aid. She had removed her shawl and I saw to my surprise that she was no woman, but a girl, with long black hair and a thin but lovely face.

"Who are you?" I asked.

"Kathleen Neal," she replied. "Mr. Neal's daughter."

I knew Tom Neal but had not met any of his children, of whom he had several. Tom Neal was one of those men who are semi-outcasts in any community in which they may live. Their independent nature and a habit of secrecy make them so. Tom Neal was a fisherman. He lived in a small cabin about two miles the other side of Spaniard's Hill. I'd exchanged a word or two with him when fishing myself. But there was no intimacy between us—nothing but a nodding acquaintance and no reason why he should have sent his daughter to help me in my plight.

"Why did you come to help me?" I asked.

She smiled, and I noted that her teeth were small and even.

"Tom of the Three Fingers told Mr. Neal to do what he could for you. Mr. Neal sent me to see what happened when the militia came to pull down your cabin. And when you rode off to Spaniard's Hill, I knew you would be trapped at the top unless I brought you to this place."

"Tom of the Three Fingers?" I cried. "But it's a week since I saw him. How could he know that I was going to get into this trouble?"

"I didn't say that he knew," said the girl. "He just asked Mr. Neal to help you if needed, and that is what has been done."

All this still did not make very much sense to me. But the girl, Kathleen, was plainly anxious to be gone and there was no time for further questioning.

"I must go now," she continued. "I'll leave the lantern with you, but you had best blow it out to save the candle. In the morning it will get light in here. There is a crevice in the top of the cave that the daylight comes through. Over there in that corner is a high place which is dry. You'll find some sheepskins to keep you warm. I will be back again in the morning."

"Could you get news to my mother that I am safe?" I asked.

She nodded gravely. "I will be able to tell you a lot more in the morning," she said and left.

In all I spent a week in that cave—a terrible lonely week which can be compared only to a week spent in a dungeon in solitary confinement. My sole relief from solitude was the girl Kathleen whom I came to look upon as a sort of angel. She brought me food and news and told me of plans for my escape to another part of Ireland. But she came only once a day and then could stay for only an hour or so.

My first night was the most terrible. My thoughts would not have permitted me to sleep even if all the other distractions such as the dripping moss, the terrible darkness and the eerie sound of the wind past the mouth of the cave had been removed. I got some comfort from the presence of the horse. At least it was alive. I could hear the beast breathing nearby, and occasionally taking a hesitant step in one direction or another. Finally I heard it settle down not far from me, and was very glad of its presence. But my thoughts were torture.

I berated myself for my attack on Lord Wedcomb which had now made me a fugitive. I wondered what was to happen to my mother and myself—particularly my mother who was without a home or support in the last years of her life. The slightest unusual sound made me start up, thinking that I had been found and was to be led off to prison.

Then, in an effort to get away from these

depressing thoughts, I began to speculate on how the girl, Kathleen, and her father had found this cave. It was not known to anyone else, of that I was sure. And for what purpose did they use it? Neal was a secretive man. I decided that he must on occasion smuggle goods in and out of Ireland and the cave served as a storehouse.

But what was the relationship between Neal and Tom of the Three Fingers—between a secretive fisherman and a tinker who roamed the length and breadth of Ireland during most of the year and made his headquarters at an inn in Dublin during the winter?

And how did Tom of the Three Fingers know that I was going to get into trouble—for he seems to have suspected some such thing, otherwise he would not have asked Neal to help me? I puzzled for a long time over that. Was it because he believed I was the one who would find the Foggy Dew and the legend said that whoever found it would go through a period of great hazard and trouble?

And then I thought of that ancestor of mine who had disappeared in a white mist one evening, with the Foggy Dew, on top of Spaniard's Hill. In the same way I had disappeared myself. And I wondered whether he also had found this cave and whether he had died in it and the Foggy Dew might not be lying somewhere around with his moldering bones.

That thought so frightened me that I did my best to drive it from my mind, but without much success. What sleep I got that first night was fitful; more of a coma than sleep, and when morning came it was to face all the fears and terrors which had been born the previous day.

When the girl, Kathleen, came in the morning, she had some news for me. A message had been sent to my mother to say that I was safe for the time being. Old Tim was dead. He had made his last charge with his pike, Liberty, and died where he fell with a musket shot through him. His cabin had been pulled down the same night as ours. The hunt was still on, with the militia led by Lord Wedcomb even now searching Spaniard's Hill over our heads and it would not be safe for me to move until the search had died down or been shifted to another area.

"But everything is not black," the girl continued. "There is some good news too. The story is going about that you have disappeared like your ancestor, Phelim O'Connor and will never be found again."

"No one is likely to believe such a story as that," I said.

"The country folk believe it already," she said. "They are refusing to help in searching the hill. Only the militia from Galway are making the search. And they are unwilling. Did you hear any noises after I left you last night?"

"Only the sounding of the wind past the mouth of the cave and the dripping of the water," I replied.

She laughed, a lovely ripple of laughter that shattered the gloominess of the cave and robbed it of much of its tomblike character.

"That wasn't the wind," she said. "Since Phelim O'Connor disappeared it has always been believed that evil spirits roam Spaniard's Hill at night. I thought to help that belief a little by standing on the hilltop and moaning and shrieking. Indeed I quite frightened myself before I was through."

We both laughed at that and I began to feel my spirits rise a little.

"Do you believe that Phelim O'Connor found this cave?" I asked. "Last night I began to think that he had died here and his bones might be lying about with the Foggy Dew somewhere beside them."

"He may have found it. And he may not," she said, looking at me steadily. "But it's certain that he did not die in the cave. Mr. Neal (she always called her father Mr. Neal) has searched every corner of this cave, and never found any trace of Phelim O'Connor or anyone else. If he did get into this cave when he disappeared, he left it again. You can be sure of that."

She came back again later that day, the first day, and took the horse away. It could not be fed in the cave and I asked what she was going to do with it.

"Mr. Neal will find a way of disposing of it," she said and would tell me no more. I missed the beast when it was gone. Now my nights were lonely indeed, and between Kathleen's visits each day, to which I looked forward with intense longing, I fell into a kind of apathy through having nothing with which to occupy my mind.

I grew weary of thinking of all my troubles and how I was to get out of them. I tried to devise some kind of clock which would tell me of the passing hours, and hit upon a fairly serviceable device. I put one of the bowls with which I had been provided under a festoon of moss from which water dripped. Then I counted the number of drops necessary to fill the bowl to the brim. It was close to four thousand, though I could not arrive at an exact figure. I estimated that a drop of water fell into the bowl every second. Thus when it was full about four thousand seconds would have passed or approximately one hour. In this way I could keep some track of the time, and it was wonderfully comforting to be able to do even so simple a thing as that.

On the fifth day, Kathleen told me that she had a message from my mother. She was well, and had been taken in by Mr. Forster, who was a bachelor and needed someone to care for him. He was a strange man. He would not advance me the two and sixpence needed to save my cabin.

But now he turned around to help my mother. There was a great deal of kindness in him, but he had a blind spot in his nature so that he could not bear to part with money.

My mother, Kathleen said, was overjoyed to know that I was well, and anxious that I should get away from Galway to some other part of Ireland, where, at a discreet time, she would be able to join me.

"And I have news for you about that, too," she said. "Tomorrow evening you will be able to leave the cave. The search for you has all but died down. Some believe, as I told you, that you disappeared like Phelim O'Connor, snatched out of life by an evil spirit. Others think that you managed under cover of the mist to elude the militia and have already gone to another part of the country. Tomorrow it will be safe to move. But it will be in the evening."

I felt now like a man who had been buried alive and was to be rescued at last. I was impatient for the hours to pass, and though I fell asleep, I would wake at some fancied sound, thinking that my liberators had come for me. When at last day came, the thought crossed my mind that perhaps I had slept through not one night, but two, and the day between, and that Kathleen had been unable to arouse me and had left me where I was. These thoughts I knew were close to insanity. Yet such was the effect of solitude and anxiety on my mind that I almost convinced myself that some such thing had happened, and started walking toward the mouth of the cave, which Kathleen had forbidden me to do.

Finally, I managed, though it took a tremendous effort, to calm myself, set my water clock, as I called the pot, in position, and watch it slowly fill with water. Whenever some natural noise occurred, like the rattling of a stone in the stream that flowed across the floor of the cave, or the scuttling of a crab (there were a number of them) in one of the corners between the floor and the wall, I would take it that Kathleen had come for me. In the end, I forced myself to sit with my back towards the entrance of the cave, and swore that I would not get up until she touched me on the shoulder and told me to come with her.

The resolve helped to steady my nerves, though I did not stick to it. When I heard her footsteps coming at last, I was on my feet, tense, my heart beating wildly. And when she was fairly in the cave and smiled and beckoned to me, I felt that there was no fairer nor more blessed human being in all the world, and that I would serve her for the rest of her life if she but asked me to.

"Come," she said holding her lantern up. And I half ran towards her and she led me out of the darkness.

CHAPTER EIGHT

THE CAVE IN WHICH I HAD SPENT the past week was midway down the face of the cliff which formed the Atlantic side of Spaniard's Hill. It was hidden from view overhead by a large boulder, and though visible from the sea appeared to be quite inaccessible from the shore below. Indeed it was inaccessible by normal methods, for there was no path up to it from the rocky beach which was covered at high tide and the cliffs falling sheer away from the cave mouth. It was a little lighter now than when I had first entered the cave and looking around at the goat track by which we had descended, and at the just visible surging of the sea some hundred feet below, I shuddered. One slip and I would have been dead.

"We must wait here a while," said Kathleen. "The boat has not come yet. But we can get ready. You can help me." She went behind the big boulder and lying there was a large block and tackle, such as is used with a primitive derrick or crane, and a coil of stout rope.

The rope, of which there must have been three

hundred feet, was very heavy, as was the rest of the apparatus, and it took some time before I had it in place.

"Will your father be in the boat?" I asked.

"He will," she replied. "It is his fishing boat. He will take you out to a schooner lying three or four miles off in the ocean. You will go aboard her and the captain will take you to Dublin. There you must look up Tom of the Three Fingers."

"Why are you doing all this for me?" I asked.

"Ask my father when you see him," was all Kathleen would say.

From below there now came a series of soft whistles. Peering down, I could see dimly a small fishing smack bobbing near the face of the cliff.

"Are you ready?" Kathleen asked. "Then put your leg through this loop. Throw the free end of the rope down to the boat."

I did so and someone caught it and pulled it tight.

"Let them take the strain," said Kathleen. "As you go down they will let the rope up through the block. Don't be afraid. All you have to do is keep yourself away from the face of the cliff with your legs."

"Won't you be coming down?" I asked.

"No," she said. "I have to stay here to haul the rope up again and hide everything."

"This is goodbye then?"

"Yes."

"I want to thank you," I said, "but I do not know how."

"It is not needed," she replied. "Go now."

"Some time I will see you again."

"If it please God, you will perhaps," she said softly.

Up from the boat below floated the hoarse word "Hurry." I slipped over the side of the cliff, my legs through a loop in the rope. It was the strangest sensation. I was lowered into a nothingness of mist, and looking upward saw Kathleen slowly recede until her long dark hair and slender face alone were visible wreathed in fog as if she were some fairy being. Then the boat appeared strongly in view below me, and I reached out for the shroud on its one mast, grasped this, and lowered myself to the deck.

Mr. Neal helped me get out of the rope and then whistled softly three times. We untangled the free end of the rope and the sling in which I had descended, rope and sling went over the side, and he went aft to the tiller.

"Cast off," he said and another man whom I had not noticed before, he having been behind the jib, cast the mooring off the smack, her big sails filled and we eased gently out to sea.

Mr. Neal was not a communicative man, and in the voyage out to the schooner, would say very little. I thanked him for what he and his daughter had done for me and asked him why he had taken such risks for a comparative stranger.

"There wasn't much risk," he said. "Not much compared to some of the risks I've taken."

"But why did you help me at all?" I persisted.

"Because you made a stand of a kind against the English. Things will change in Ireland. It won't always be bowing and scraping. The tenants will stand up for their rights some day. You showed the way though you didn't succeed. You were worth saving. If you'd been caught and hung or jailed, the day when the others made their stand would be postponed. You had to be saved."

"Is there to be a rising?" I asked.

To this Mr. Neal said nothing for such an interval that I concluded that he had decided not to answer the question. Then, when I had about given up, he said, as if addressing his remarks to the mainsail or the mist around, "No. There won't be a rising. No organized rising. When there's an organization, the English have an enemy they can come to grips with and wipe out. There'll just be resistance, individual resistance like yours all over Ireland. That way the English won't be able to get to grips with one enemy. They'll be fighting the whole population individually. They can't win that kind of a fight. Nobody can win that kind of a fight."

Another question now occurred to me. "What happened to the horse?" I asked.

"It was sold in France," he said quietly.

"In France?" If he had said it had been sent to the moon on a broomstick I could hardly have been more surprised.

"In France," said Mr. Neal. "Many horses from Ireland are sold in France. The French aren't particular who owns them." Still holding the tiller with one hand, he lifted the rough fisherman's jersey which covered him from neck to waist and fumbled in a money belt. He took out five gold sovereigns and gave them to me.

"Here's your share of the sale," he said. "The rest I kept for my trouble."

I knew now that Mr. Neal was certainly a smuggler, and used the cave for his activities. The block and tackle arrangement was a good one either for landing goods from the sea, or getting them away in a boat. Yet I was astonished that he had been able to lower the horse from the cave down to his boat, for I had not thought the tackle would be strong enough.

"We used other tackle," he said in reply to my question on the subject. "The ring in the boulder is stout enough for the work. And there's nothing to lowering a horse down—or cows for that matter. A sling and a couple of bales of straw on either side of them to stop their getting hurt against the cliff is all that is needed. We can lower away by the winch up forward."

"Ship ahoy," said the other man who was standing by the mast under the lee of the mainsail.

"Your passage is paid for to Dublin," said Mr. Neal. "When I bring the smack alongside the schooner, get aboard as fast as you can. She's French. Say nothing to anybody and there'll be no questions asked. And good luck to you." He held out his hand and hushed my attempts at thanks.

"When you see Tom of the Three Fingers at the 'Whistling Goat' give him a message for me," he said. "The message is this: 'Captain Moonlight must go a-hunting.' Can you remember it?"

" 'Captain Moonlight must go a-hunting,' " I repeated.

"Good. All right. Get ready."

"One thing more," I said. "I don't need all this money. Can you get four of these sovereigns to my mother?"

"Don't worry about her," said Mr. Neal. "The horse fetched a good price. Away with you."

While talking he had brought the sloop very neatly indeed alongside the schooner and on her lee. Her deck was no more than a foot or so above ours, and I was able, by climbing a short way up the main shrouds of the sloop and taking advantage of a favorable roll of the vessel, to jump safely aboard. Mr. Neal and his man immediately pushed off and the fishing smack disappeared in the mist.

We were but two days fetching Dublin, and during that time I had little but perfunctory talks with the crew of the schooner, which was called *La République*. Nobody asked me any questions about myself and none volunteered any information about the schooner which I certainly believed was engaged in the smuggling trade, though it was ostensibly a deep-water fishing boat.

I went ashore as soon as the vessel docked, and set out to find the "Whistling Goat" where I could expect to meet Tom of the Three Fingers again.

Dublin was a strange city then, knowing only two kinds of residence. There were beautiful houses with marble steps before them, heavy carved doors and pillars supporting a porch in the Greek style. And there were little hovels of brick and wood and tarred paper, often no more than a street away from these noble mansions. The hovels lined mean streets full of filth and discarded rubbish of every kind. Some of these streets were so narrow that a carriage could not be driven down them, and cobbles had been pulled up for building material, so that the streets were often mere ditches of mud and foul water.

It was the work of almost half a day to find the "Whistling Goat." I thought that being a tavern, it would stand out from the wretched habitations around. But here I was mistaken. It was itself little more than a hovel—its signboard a weathered and broken piece of wood fastened to the wall.

And the tavern itself was of such ramshackle construction that it could not have stood up but for the support of the buildings on either side of it.

Like many Dublin houses near the waterfront the front door was so low that I had to stoop to go through it, and the wooden walls were littered with posters and notices of all kinds and ages, nailed there but never taken down so that these notices formed a sort of outer skin for the building. I looked at some of the notices before entering. The greater part dealt with the departure of fast packets for America, the price of passage being as low as a pound on some, and the accommodations invariably described as "luxurious." It seemed that no packet left Ireland for America which did not promise "luxurious comfort" for passengers, "Speedy transportation," "Dry sleeping quarters," and food if needed.

Among these notices were others offering rewards for the apprehension of criminals, sailors who had jumped ship, the return of articles lost but believed stolen, and so on. These reward notices gave me a flush of anxiety. I feared that there might be one offering a reward for my own capture, and I plunged through the door feeling very guilty.

It took me a few minutes to get accustomed to the gloom of the small room in which I now found myself. Being devoid of windows, it was lit by one lantern, burning whale oil, which hung from a nail on one of the walls. There was a counter at the end of this small room, facing the door through which I had come, and at it three scarecrows of human beings, playing dice. One of them was smoking a short clay pipe, and the tobacco filled the room with a heavy reek.

All three turned around to examine me as I entered. The one who was smoking the pipe came over to me slowly and with a certain air of challenge and looked me up and down. "Who are you?" he asked.

"Kevin O'Connor," I replied.

"As good a name as any," said the pipe smoker. "Where are you from?"

"What business of that is yours?" I asked, for I did not like his attitude.

"Do you hear that now?" said the pipe smoker, turning to his two companions. " 'What business of that is yours?' he asks. Well, I'll tell you now. It's no business of mine at all." With that, he burst out laughing, though I do not know for what reason, and then stopped abruptly. "But I'm making it my business," he said. "Now where are you from and quick about it!"

"Ah leave him alone," said one of the men at the counter. "Maybe he'll buy us a jar, for I'm as dry as summer dust this morning."

"Will you now?" said the pipe smoker. "Will you buy a jar of porter apiece—it's to be had for two-pence—to help make yourself welcome?"

"Gladly," I said, for I wanted no trouble.

"Andrew," roared the pipe smoker. "Andrew! Tumble out of bed there. We've got a live one." There was some kind of commotion from behind the counter, and a man raised his head above it.

"Four jars," said the pipe smoker. "Come on over and I'll introduce you to my friends."

His friends' names were Tom and Bill—names so obviously assumed that I did not pay any attention to which was which. As for himself, he said I could call him Dick.

"I'm looking for Tom of the Three Fingers," I said to Andrew when he had awakened sufficiently to bring us the porter. "Do you know him?"

"I do," said Andrew.

"Is he here?" I asked.

"That depends." He eyed the change from the shilling with which I had paid for the porter. I pushed it towards him. "I want to speak with Tom of the Three Fingers," I said.

"Speak to him you shall," said Andrew, pocketing the coins. "I can see that you're a gentleman. Not like some." He cast a black look at the three men who had called themselves Bill, Tom, and Dick and, nodding to me, told me to follow him behind the counter.

CHAPTER NINE

TOM OF THE THREE FINGERS was delighted to see me and not a whit surprised. He had a small room as a lodging in the inn and it was to this that I was taken by the man, Andrew. It lay at the top of a flight of stairs at the back of the house, stairs so ancient that each tread groaned as I stood upon it and the whole threatened to collapse, it seemed, at any moment.

"Kevin O'Connor!" said Tom as the man Andrew showed me into his room. "Well, you're not a day early."

"You were expecting me?" I asked, surprised.

"I was," he said taking his bit of pipe off the top of a grubby mantle. "I was indeed."

"I don't understand," I said.

"Arrah," he said, "when I spoke to your mother the day I was at your cabin, I knew you were short of the rent, and I suspected there would be trouble. You'll recall that I told you to look for me in Dublin if you were in need of a friend. And here you are. But sit down on the bed there and tell me what has been happening to you and what I can

76

do for you. Ruby," he said to his dog, "go outside now and see that we have no visitors." The aged animal got up with a certain air of surliness and went out the door, to crouch on the small landing outside.

"Extra eyes and ears for me is Ruby," said Tom. He seated himself in a small wicker rocking chair, which with the truckle bed formed the only furniture of the room, and awaited my story.

I told him all that had happened and he did not once interrupt me.

"Ah," he said when I had finished. "It's harsh times that are coming for the people of Galway. And for the people of the rest of Ireland for that matter. But especially in Galway for the new Lord Wedcomb is a harsh man, proud and arrogant and determined to wipe out the tenantry."

He looked at me in a queer calculating way for a moment or two. "Did Mr. Neal send any message to me by you?" he asked.

"Yes," I replied. "His message was 'Captain Moonlight must go a-hunting.' It doesn't make any sense to me, but that's what he said."

" 'Captain Moonlight must go a-hunting,' " repeated Tom. "Well now, that's very interesting. Very interesting indeed. And it's a message that concerns you though you don't see the connection yet.

"Kevin, me boy," he continued, "have you ever heard of the Young Irelanders?" I shook my head.

"Well, it's no matter," said Tom. "They're an organization dedicated to the freedom of Ireland —by any method possible, not stopping short of murder.

"They're strong here in Dublin, and their intention is to get the land back from the English landlords and give it to their Irish tenants. They'll make a start on Lord Wedcomb. He's to be shot by Captain Moonlight and that in the near future."

"Captain Moonlight," I cried. "Who is Captain Moonlight?"

"Why," said Tom, "Captain Moonlight's everybody and nobody in a manner of speaking. He might even be you."

"Me?" I cried.

"The same," said Tom.

There was a shocked silence while I wrestled to make some sense out of this conversation. I gathered that Lord Wedcomb was to be assassinated; that whoever the assassin was, he would be known by the name of Captain Moonlight. And then it came clearly to me. I was chosen to be the assassin.

"I can't do it," I cried. "I can't shoot a man in cold blood."

"He'd shoot you with no more concern than he would shoot a fox," said Tom. "There's a price on your head. You're a fugitive from the law. You are to be captured, dead or alive."

"I don't care," I said. "I can't kill him. And

even if I did, that wouldn't help me. I'd be hunted more than ever."

"My boy," said Tom, "you're young and don't know much of the ways of the world. It isn't all justice, plain black and white like in the school-books. A boy by himself, with a price on his head, which is your situation, has few friends, and can't afford to offend those who take his side. The Young Irelanders have befriended you. You must look to your own interests first and those of your mother, and put aside your scruples. Scruples are no comfort to a man cold in his grave. Play Captain Moonlight for the Young Irelanders on this occasion and we'll get you clean away to France—your mother, too—and with money in your pocket to start a new life. Or we can put you on a packet to America. It's a fine country and no one can touch you there."

"No," I said. "I can't do it."

"It's a pity," said Tom. "A great pity. Mind you, I'm your friend now. Always bear that in mind. But I'm not in the driver's seat in this matter. Not by a long chalk. There's those higher than me and those higher than them. But if I were to say to those above me that you refused to play Captain Moonlight, do you know what would happen?"

"No," I said.

"They'd turn you over to the police and there'd be nothing I could do to help you."

At that my heart sank. I was trapped. The people I thought were friends, Mr. Neal the smuggler, and Tom the tinker, only saw me as a tool. If I refused to work for them, they would betray me.

"But Lord Wedcomb's in Galway," I said, clinging to straws. "You don't expect me to go back there with the whole countryside looking for me?"

"He has a fine house here in Dublin," said Tom. "On the other side of Phoenix Park. Wedcomb House. He'll be back there tomorrow afternoon according to my information."

How Tom knew this I could not then guess, beyond the fact that in his wanderings around the country, he played the part of a spy or agent of the Young Irelanders, and must have a hundred sources of news in a score of different parts.

"What is it I am to do?" I asked miserably.

"You've a good head on your shoulders, I can see that," said Tom. "You know where your own best interests lie. Never forget to look after your own interests as I said before, my boy.

"Now, here's what is to happen. Lord Wedcomb will be coming to Dublin by coach tomorrow night. Of that I'm sure. His coach will take the road through Phoenix Park. And there's a place where the road passes through some elm trees with plenty of cover for you to hide in. The road is full of bends and twists, so the horses will be at a walk. All you have to do is shoot him as soon as he comes into view. Then send a volley at the horses and get back here. From then on, we'll take care of you."

"How will you take care of me?" I demanded.

"You'll be on a ship bound for France in half an hour with fifty guineas in your pocket. You'll be away before the search is properly on. You'll be landed at Brest two days later, and go to an address which I will give you. Wait there for a day or two and your mother will join you. Then you can decide whether to go to America or remain in France. The whole world will be yours to roam in and you'll be away free with all your troubles behind you."

"Why should I trust you?" I asked. "How do I know that afterwards you won't turn me over to the police anyway?"

"To tell you the truth," said Tom, "there's no way I can assure you beyond giving my word. But look at it this way. If you don't play Captain Moonlight, why then, you'll be in jail tomorrow instead of around free. On that you can rely. So you must reckon the odds. Jail for sure, a quick trial, and a quick hanging for they'll make the gravest case they can against you. Or the chance of a free getaway if you do just this one job. I'm not the only one who knows you are in Dublin, you know. There are others."

"You mean Tom, Dick, and Bill?" I asked.

"The same," said Tom.

As I saw it then, I had no alternative. I nodded my head in miserable agreement.

"Good," said Tom springing up. "We'll go out now and over to Phoenix Park so you'll know which way the coach will come and where is the best place to set your ambush."

The day was beautiful—a return almost of summer. But the brightness of the sunshine, the sleepy warmth of the dusty grass and leaves in the park, the chirping of the sparrows, and the quick darting of squirrels up the trunks of trees as we approached, all seemed remote and unreal to me. I felt like a man condemned to death, taking his last look upon the world, and finding that it had already halfway gone from him. Even the people in the streets and the traffic of handcarts, horses and carriages, seemed to have no true substance. Our way lay along Patrick Street, past the cathedral and castle, and so on to the park. When we came near the park, we passed a barracks of the British Horse Guards, and here Tom of the Three Fingers spat copiously upon the road.

"There's many an Irish lad has gone through those gates to enlist," he said, "and never been heard of again. I'm told they use them for target practice."

Finally we got to the park where the road ran in a series of twists through the grove of elms. "As fine a spot for the activities of Captain Moonlight as is to be found in all Ireland," said Tom very cheerfully. "Now you see that little rise in the ground there? That's the place for you. Come on over and you'll see that you'd have a good view into any carriage that was coming along the road in either direction."

He took me over and showed me how, lying down, I would not be seen from the road, but would still be able to fire into the carriage and kill Lord Wedcomb. "Then," he said, "one round for the horses—you'll have a two-barrel shotgun for the work and the range is no more than fifty feet. One round for the horses to stampede them. Then leave the gun and off with you."

In my mind I could already see the dreadful scene: Lord Wedcomb's arrogant golden head covered with blood, and the horses pelting down the road carrying him along as he died. I sought desperately for some method of talking my way out of the plan.

"But what about the gun?" I asked. "I can't be seen walking through the city in daylight carrying a gun in my hands."

"It's a good head you have on your shoulders, as I remarked before," said Tom. "I've a fancy that you have a talent for this kind of work. Not that we intend to use you any more than once," he added quickly. "You'll come here without the gun. And here's where you'll find it." He led me to a thicket of hawthorn near the little rise where I was to lie in ambush.

"It will be right here," he said. "Fully charged with heavy shot so that at this range you can't fail to kill him. When you've done your job, run for it back to the inn. It'll be dark, eight o'clock in the evening or thereabouts and very few people in the park. So there's no chance at all of you being found if you just get away fast."

"And now," he concluded, "you know everything. And no doubt you're hungry. We'll get a bite to eat and spend the rest of the day walking around the city and seeing the sights." He prattled on about all the sights which were to be seen, but his words were quite meaningless to me. I felt myself doomed with no place to turn; an outlaw, who to save himself, must commit a murder.

CHAPTER TEN

THE FOLLOWING EVENING I WAS EARLY at the post of murder picked out for me so cheerfully by Tom of the Three Fingers. During the night, spent with him at his room at the "Whistling Goat," I had gone over in my mind a hundred plans for avoiding the role of assassin to which I had been assigned. Indeed, I had resolved that I would pretend to be quite ready to shoot Lord Wedcomb, but I would just disappear into the city of Dublin instead, after having gone to the park.

But that plan was very efficiently foiled when Tom went to the park with me. "I'll be over in the clump of trees there, near at hand," he said, "in case of any trouble." So that was that. I'd no doubt that he would keep a careful watch on me to make sure that I did not move. And if I did not shoot, I would, without a doubt, be handed over to the police. Or perhaps he would shoot me. He had a large horse pistol with him.

There remained for me then but one escape. That was to shoot but miss. It is strange that this did not occur to me until I was lying on the small hill overlooking the road along which Lord Wedcomb's coach was to come. If I shot but missed, I could not be blamed. There would be no way to prove that I had missed on purpose, although that might be suspected. Still there was a reasonable chance that I would not be handed over to the police, but would be permitted to go on my way.

Yet there seemed some flaw in my thinking here. I was aware that I had not got hold of all the pieces of this murder plot. But I could not think what was the missing piece. Then, suddenly, it came to me, and left me cold with fear.

Of course Tom had thought of the possibility that I would deliberately miss! But that wasn't important. He wouldn't. He would fire with his horse pistol at Lord Wedcomb and he would shoot to kill.

Yet if he had intended to shoot Lord Wedcomb himself, why had he brought me into the matter? For a while I could get no answer to this. The answer I hit upon was terrible. When I fled the scene of the crime—if indeed I got away—and arrived at the "Whistling Goat," Tom would not be there. More likely there would be British agents at the inn tipped off by Tom, who would take me. The crime of murder would be pinned on me, and no member of the organization called the Young Irelanders would be touched. Since

Lord Wedcomb had pulled down our cabin, a motive would be easily established. In short, I was to be the dupe, the scapegoat.

I cannot describe the panic which filled me when I realized this. It was as if I were looking into my own grave, preparing to pitch headlong into it and unable to stop myself. For a while I was quite incapable of clear thought. The instinct to jump to my feet and run; to run anywhere, was almost overpowering.

"Kevin, are ye there, me boy?" Tom's voice called out to me from the darkness across the road.

"Yes," I replied.

"Good lad," he said. " 'Twill only be half an hour now. I'll stay with you. But don't look for me here after the shooting. Just make straight for the 'Whistling Goat.' And no more talk until it's done."

Half an hour. If I was to do anything at all, I would have to do it right away. Not knowing quite what I intended, I got on my hands and knees, leaving the double-barreled shotgun on the ground. I went stealthily away from the hill top, down to a kind of little dell, and, rising, hurried along this to where I knew it joined the road further up. This little journey of no more than twenty yards seemed to me to take an hour. But action, just getting up and moving, cleared my mind for me, and when I got to the road, around a bend from where Tom lay in ambush, I knew

87

what I must do. I must intercept Lord Wedcomb's coach and tell him of the ambush ahead.

I set out running along the grass beside the road until, after perhaps fifteen minutes, I came within sight of the gates of the park where Lord Wedcomb's coach would enter. As I did so I heard the rumble of the wheels of the heavy coach and the next second, four blood horses turned through the gate with an overland coach behind them. I knew that this must be Lord Wedcomb's vehicle and I ran swiftly to the center of the road and stood there, waving my arms and calling upon the coachman to stop.

It was so dark that I do not believe the coachman saw me until he was just a few feet away. Whether he heard me or not, over the noise of the wheels and the thunder of the horses' hooves, I do not know. Certainly he paid me no attention. Rather he laid his whip to the horses which plunged straight for me, and I just managed to throw myself aside and avoid being trampled to death. The coach had gone by in the next second, headed for the spot perhaps half a mile away, where Tom lay in ambush.

My one desire now was to get out of the park and away from the assassination scene. I had done what I could to save Lord Wedcomb, and must save myself. But where was I to go? The Young Irelanders would certainly be looking for me. Tipped off by Tom—if he survived the night's work—the police would be looking for me also. There was nowhere to turn, nowhere at all. I was helpless and without a friend anywhere.

I was by now out of the park and pelting down the street which ran alongside of it. I steadied sufficiently to realize that running as I was, I must draw suspicion upon myself and forced myself to slow down to a walk. And then I saw ahead a light outside of a building, and a small crowd of people standing around. My desire to be lost among my fellow beings was so strong that without thinking further, I joined this little crowd.

It was some time before I realized what they were there for. A sergeant of hussars was seated before a table and had a long sheet of paper before him. There were two troopers with him, all very splendidly dressed but by no means cutting a military figure. Instead, they were drinking tankards of porter and had several black bottles of the stuff on the table. Nor was the sergeant in any stiff parade ground attitude. He also had a tankard of porter, and the three of them seemed to be enjoying themselves very much indeed.

At the moment I arrived, the sergeants had just given a penny to a fiddler and bidden him to strike up with the "Rakes of Mallow" and the tune went briskly with the three hussars keeping time to it with their tankards.

"Come now, my brave bullies," said the sergeant when the tune was finished. "Who'll join me in a toast to the Queen? Fill up the tankards there, trooper. Hussar's measure—a pint for the man and another for his horse! Two pints of best porter free for anyone who'll toast the Queen with me."

Several tankards were filled and passed around. But there seemed a remarkable reluctance on the part of any in the crowd to accept them, despite the assurance that the drink was free. One of the troopers pressed a tankard into my hands and I accepted it with some surprise.

"Don't drink it," said a man standing next to me.

"Why?" I asked.

"There'll be the Queen's shilling in the bottom," replied the man.

"The Queen's shilling?"

"You must be from the country," said the man. "If you drink it and there's a shilling in the bottom, it will be taken that you've accepted the Queen's shilling. And you'll be in the army."

"Is that what they're here for?" I asked.

"Why, sure it is," said the man. "There's rumors of a war and the Tenth Hussars are recruiting to bring themselves up to strength. I'm warning you. If you drink that porter, you'll be in the army the very next second."

"All right now, my bullies," said the sergeant. "Raise your tankards and drink the Queen's health." He raised his own and so did the other troopers. But none in the crowd joined him.

"Come," said the sergeant, glowering around quite fiercely, as if poorly treated by people whom he had come to regard as friends and comrades, "is there none among you who will take a free drink of porter to the health of Her Majesty Queen Victoria the First?—God bless her."

"I will," I said.

"Ah, there's a brave bucko and a loyal subject," said the sergeant. "I'm glad to see there's some spirit around. All right, my boy, to the Queen, God bless her." With that he and the troopers raised their tankards and I drank with them.

"To the bottom," said the sergeant.

"I can't make it in one go," I replied.

"Well, keep on trying, you must drink it all up."

It took me several swallows to get the bitter thick stuff down, and when I did, it was to find a shilling in the bottom of the tankard as the man had warned me.

"Well, my boy," said the sergeant, as I tipped the shilling out into my hand, "you've taken the Queen's shilling in the presence of two witnesses of her Majesty's forces. You're in the army now."

I think he expected me to remonstrate and perhaps run for it, for the two troopers had moved over so as to be on either side of me.

"I'm glad of it," I said.

91

"You're what?" said the sergeant.

"I'm glad," I repeated.

"Well by thunder,' said the sergeant. "I never thought to hear those words in Dublin. You must be from the country."

"I am," I replied. "And I'm anxious to get into the army as soon as possible."

"What your reasons may be," the sergeant replied, "I don't know and I don't care. What's your name?"

"Kevin O'Connor," I replied.

"County?"

"Galway," I said before I could stop myself, and was dismayed when I uttered the word. Surely the army would know that Kevin O'Connor of Galway was wanted as a fugitive from justice. But the sergeant didn't seem to mind.

"Kevin O'Connor, Galway," he said as he wrote it down on the sheet of paper on the table.

"Father's name?"

"Michael O'Connor. He died in the potato famine."

"Mother's name?"

"Sinaid O'Connor."

"Dead?"

"No."

"Where does she live?"

At this I hesitated. If I gave the address of my mother, which was care of Mr. Forster, in Galway

City, that would be positive identification of myself.

"I don't know, sir," I said.

"Address unknown at the time of enlistment," said the sergeant, writing it down. He took some more information and when he had done, read an oath for me so fast that I could hardly hear the words. There was something about swearing to lay down my life in defense of the Queen if my duty bade me. That done, the sergeant gave me the sheet of paper and told me to sign my name at the bottom of the entry concerning myself.

When I had done this I looked up from the table and got a start. Standing almost opposite me was Tom of the Three Fingers. I could feel the blood drain away from my face and was quite sure he was going to denounce me as a fugitive from justice. But what he said was quite different. "Well, Kevin, my boy," he said, "you've done it. You've joined the army."

"Yes," I replied feebly.

"And a very good thing too," said Tom. "You've a good head on your shoulders as I remarked before. 'Look after yourself first of all,' I told you and I see that's exactly what you've done."

"You know this recruit?" asked the sergeant.

"Known him since he didn't have to stoop to roll a turnip," said Tom. "Known him and loved him."

If I'd had a knife handy I'd have stuck it in his

cold heart for the sanctimonious way in which he said that.

"Well, perhaps there are some other brave lads, you've known since childhood, you could persuade to join up," said the sergeant.

"No," said Tom. "No. There are none in quite the same circumstances, with quite the same reasons as young Kevin here." And he gave me a look full of meaning.

"Might I inquire," he continued, "what regiment the boy will be assigned to?"

"The Tenth Hussars," said the sergeant.

"The Tenth Hussars," repeated Tom. "Now isn't that a wonderful stroke of luck? A wonderful stroke of luck indeed. Am I right now, sergeant, in saying that the Tenth Hussars are commanded by Lord Wedcomb?"

"You are," said the sergeant.

"Ah," said Tom. "A fine soldierly figure is Lord Wedcomb. Though harsh they say. A stickler for discipline. When I saw him last he was in the very best of health."

With that he gave me a short bob of his head and slipped off into the night.

CHAPTER ELEVEN

THE FIRST FOUR MONTHS OF MY LIFE as a cavalry recruit were so arduous, so full of unremitting activity punctuated by only slight periods of rest for food or sleep, that I wonder to this day that I survived them.

The civilian who becomes a soldier, I soon discovered, abandons what little rights he may have had in previous years. He abandons them utterly to whatever non-commissioned officer is immediately over him. He becomes a mere cipher to whom no consideration need be extended, a cipher which can appeal against no injustice or hardship; a cipher which must become capable of bearing every kind of repression and hazing and maltreatment without show of anger, resentment, sorrow, or indeed any emotion.

The non-commissioned officer to whose iron discipline and all-seeing eyes I was to be subject during my training period was Corporal Baggins. He was a big, fleshy-faced, pop-eyed man, with a set of fearsome mustaches always glistening with wax. It was a common rumor among the recruits at the training barracks in Dublin that he wore a corset.

I recall two especial characteristics of the man. The first that he was a perfect stranger to the letter "h." There was no such letter in the alphabet for him and that being the case, he made no use of it. "Horses" were " 'orses" for Corporal Baggins, "hooves," " 'ooves," and "hackles," " 'ackles." Nonetheless he was under the impression that he spoke English perfectly and that all who could not understand him were halfwits.

His second peculiarity was the foulness of his breath. I will not dwell upon this beyond stating that it was his custom when dressing a recruit down—that is to say, bawling him out—to thrust his face within an inch of the offender's nose and heap verbal abuse of remarkable force upon him. On such occasion, it was difficult to decide which was the most painful—the corporal's breath or the corporal's words. But no recruit dared flinch from one or the other of them.

Corporal Baggins had been with the cavalry since Waterloo where he had been a trooper in the Inniskilling Dragoons, taking part in the famous charge of Lord Uxbridge's cavalry into the mass of the French. For this he had received a medal (represented by a faded blue ribbon on his tunic) and the rank of corporal. It might be said of him that his life had achieved its fullest flood at the moment when the dragoons raced into the French ranks some forty years previously. All that followed that event was mere anticlimax. For him there was no battle in all history greater than Waterloo and no action in any battle to parallel the charge of the Inniskilling Dragoons and the Scots Greys on that day.

All recruits were compared to his comrades of that battle and found woefully lacking, and Corporal Baggins' most trenchant criticism of a recruit was to say, with withering scorn, that a few more like the offender in Wellington's army and Napoleon would have won the day. Under this stern and unbending warrior, whose bellow was more frightening to me than a discharge of heavy artillery, I struggled bemused, miserable, nerve wracked, and dead tired along the painful road from civilian to recruit, from recruit to trooper.

After some days, I became convinced that I was capable of doing nothing right; that my mere presence was sufficient to boggle up the simplest situation. I could not carry a bucket of water without slopping some on my boots—an unforgivable offense. I could not mix a bran of crushed oats and oil cake without getting the proportions completely wrong. I quickly learned that the noblest of all beasts, far higher in the scheme of things than mere man, was the horse. Man, himself, at least as far as cavalry recruits were concerned, had been put upon earth for the purpose of serving horses, currying them, brushing them, watering them, feeding them, polishing their hooves, cleaning out their bedding and renewing it, combing their manes, and tails, and removing their dung. And in all this relationship the horse could do no wrong. Man was the only sinner.

I spent countless hours upon these duties and then countless more cleaning the accoutrements of the horse. The metal of the harness, though but steel, had to take on all the high fire of diamonds. Bits had to be cleaned, polished, and kept clean and polished. The same for stirrups. Reins and saddles and girths had to have the deep smooth luster of old mahogany. Saddle blankets had to be cleaner than the single blanket with which I was provided for my own bed. The horse blankets with which we covered the horses were of a wool far superior and a weave far more soft than our own.

I can tell you that when I started I had some love of horses, and a way with them, which was why Mr. Forster the farrier had given me a little employment during the hunting season in Galway. But after a few weeks at the training barracks, I loathed horses. The very word "horse," or " 'orse" as I heard it more often, filled me with slow anger. Much has been written about the affection between horses and men. But most of it was written by people who had someone else to do the stable work.

I have dwelt here on the long hours of what

might be called waiting on horses. But that was the mere base of the matter, the foundation upon which the rest was built. For quite as great a part of my work was taken up with learning to ride horses and drill with them. And for this purpose the Tenth Hussars had a wicked beast known as The Major. The Major was a big, stiff-legged animal, gray colored, yellow eyed, yellow toothed, and evil tempered. He had a habit of biting any who came near him, and his bites were not playful nips but vicious, cunning attacks.

This evil creature, whose heart seemed always black with intent of murder, was the chosen instrument for teaching recruits in the Tenth Hussars to ride and especially to jump. The Major could not be used for drill because he invariably snapped the tail of the horse ahead. But solo he was a star performer.

In those days all horsemanship was taught barebacked, without benefit of saddle or spurs, it being assumed that if a man could handle a horse without a saddle, he could certainly handle one which was fully equipped with harness. We recruits were compelled to mount The Major and ride him barebacked around the barracks yard at a walk, a trot, a canter, and a gallop. It was not sufficient to stay on his back and by keeping an iron grip on the reins, prevent him turning around and snapping at your knees. All must be performed with the rider sitting upright and stiff as a poker, the elbows tucked into the side, the sword arm hanging down free, the soles of the feet sloping from toe to heel toward the ground.

Riding The Major then was a daily ordeal for me, an ordeal which was refined, as the days went by and I acquired more mastery over him, by the addition of jumping. For this exercise the brute was mercifully muzzled, for the rider had to learn to jump without benefit of reins or saddle, and with his arms held behind his back. The reason was that a horse, whether in plain riding or jumping, is largely controlled by the pressure of the legs of the rider against his side. In jumping, the rider balances the horse by shifting his own weight, leaning forward at the takeoff and back at the landing. He urges the horse at the fence by the pressure of his legs, and must give him a free head—hence, no reins. I couldn't count the number of spills I took at the jumping exercises. Every muscle was bruised. Every bone ached. It was considered a show of cowardice, even when falling from the horse, to unclasp one's hands before hitting the ground.

With all of this there was of course drill in the company of other members of the troop, riding in column, two files of riders and horses and then at a flourish of the bugle swinging into line, charging, wheeling, retreating, counter-charging, and all this over plain ground, broken ground, undulating ground, plowed fields, areas strewn with boulders and clumps of gorse until there was no aspect of the work of a cavalryman which I did not know in detail.

In all this I was haunted by two fears. The first that it would be discovered that I was a fugitive and would be handed over to the civil authorities for trial; the second that I would meet the colonel of the regiment, Lord Wedcomb, who would recognize me and wreak his personal vengeance upon me, for he had power of life and death over every man under his command.

On the first score, my fears abated after a while, largely as a result of conversation with my fellow recruits. A large number of them were wanted in civil life for some offense or other. Some of the offenses were trivial—non-payment of debts being a common cause. The debtors prison was escaped by the simple expedient of going to another kind of prison—the army. Others were more serious. A recruit who became a special friend of mine admitted that he was wanted in County Mayo for killing a gamekeeper.

The recruit's name was Peter Storey. He was a gangling man, all bone and sinew. The gamekeeper had set a mantrap, that is a spring gun which discharged and killed whoever was unlucky enough to pass before it. The device was perfectly legal under the laws aimed at preventing poaching, for more was thought of the preservation of partridges and hares than the destruction of poachers. The trap had wounded a friend of Peter's and Peter had sought the gamekeeper intending to give him a good beating. But it had ended in Peter killing the gamekeeper with the latter's gun, and although the killing was an accident, Peter had fled and joined the army.

Probably because he was in the same position as I—a fugitive from the law on a serious charge —Peter and I became great friends. We found a sort of spiritual kinship and spent as much time as we could together. I told him my own story, with some hesitation, but glad to be able to tell it to someone. He made light of it all.

"Why," he said, "half the people in Ireland are wanted for some offense or another. We've become a nation of lawbreakers and that because there are too many laws against us. When the greater number of people in any country are lawbreakers and fugitives from justice, then it is not the people who need changing but the laws. The people are right and the laws wrong."

These statements, made slowly and simply, were a revelation to me. I had always thought of the law, however harsh it might be, as superior to any man. But could there not be a condition such as existed in Ireland, when the laws themselves instead of promoting good produced evil and so should be swept away? I thought many times about this, and felt somewhat better about my own situation.

Largely then as a result of my friendship with Peter, and the discovery of the number of my fellows wanted for some offense or the other, my first fear, of being handed over to the civil authorities, gradually diminished and finally left me. But my second fear, that of meeting with Lord Wedcomb in whose regiment I was a common soldier, stayed with me day and night. It troubled my sleep as much as it troubled my waking hours, and even Peter, who tried to assure me that his lordship never once glanced at the face of a recruit, could not console me. I knew that one day his lordship would come face to face with me. And I knew that he would take a particular revenge upon me for the beating I gave him at my cabin. I knew also that he had unlimited power to take that revenge.

The dreaded meeting occurred one month after joining the Tenth Hussars. Lord Wedcomb had purchased the commission of colonel with command of the regiment by the payment of sixty thousand pounds. This was a fact known to everybody connected with the hussars. That he had no previous military experience, that he had nothing in his background to justify his being corporal let alone a colonel, made no difference. He had the two qualifications then deemed necessary to purchase a commission—wealth and a title. Military experience counted as nothing.

The night he came to Dublin—the night that

I was to have assassinated him—his purpose had been to take over officially command of the Tenth Hussars. This had been done in a ceremony in which I took no part as a recruit of but a few hours' service. Lord Wedcomb had then gone on to London, among other things to have a new uniform designed for the Tenth Hussars and get an even more splendid uniform for himself.

The day of his return was marked by a series of orders signed by Wedcomb and covering the minutest aspects of our lives. His lordship had observed that troopers stabling horses were in the habit of removing their jackets and working in their shirt sleeves. This would not be tolerated. Troopers must be smart in appearance and properly dressed no matter the duty upon which they were engaged.

His lordship had observed that it was customary to water several horses at one time from a common trough. This was to be discontinued immediately. It made a mess in the watering area, horses were liable to communicate disease one to the other, and furthermore some horses got insufficent water. In future, all mounts would be watered in their stalls from buckets.

This added enormously to the work of the troopers. But there was more to come. His lordship had noted that only two men mounted guard on the stable areas at night. The guard should be increased to at least a dozen. His lordship wished half a dozen mounted guards on duty at all hours outside the barracks. The habit of sending unmounted men on sentry duty, with boxes to protect them from the weather was downright slovenly and unsoldierly.

So it was that half a dozen troopers had to stand sentry duty in the driving rain, snow, or bitter frost, seated rigid upon horses which became chilled to the bone, for we were now approaching the height of winter. The horses naturally became sick. But that did not worry his lordship. Indeed nothing worried his lordship except the possibility that there was an order which he had not issued, or that some scruple of one of his orders was not being carried out.

Even Corporal Baggins, as loyal a soldier as it was possible to find, received a dressing down from Lord Wedcomb (who had never heard a shot fired in anger) for what was termed slovenliness —the slovenliness consisting of a stable bucket being found on its bracket with a little water in the bottom of it.

This was the tyrant then who set out to destroy me mentally or physically. And he had the power to do both.

CHAPTER TWELVE

LORD WEDCOMB DISCOVERED MY PRESENCE in his regiment when I was on sentry duty one day outside the barracks. Since he was determined that six mounted men should perform this duty at all hours of the day and night, he made a habit of inspecting the guard personally at irregular hours. His lordship had no faith at all in the willingness or the ability of his officers to carry out their orders. He found it necessary to check on them constantly.

It was three in the afternoon of a particularly foul day when his lordship decided to inspect the outside guard of which I formed a part. Accompanied by his aide-de-camp, Captain Witherton Spenlove-Smith, he came wheeling through the barracks gate to the area outside where we were on duty, mounted upon a hunter and tricked out in full regimentals. He passed by each man of the guard, inspecting his equipment closely until he came to me. He looked me over from my boots through every detail of my dress and the equipment of my horse until at last, for a second, his eyes lit on my face. His face drained white with anger which for a little while left him quite speechless.

Finally he bellowed, "Captain Smith, what is this blackguard doing in my regiment?"

"My Lord?" said Captain Smith, utterly bewildered.

"This confounded cowardly rascal," roared his lordship, the end of his riding crop pressed against my chest. "He's wanted through the length and breadth of the country as a notorious troublemaker, inciting the tenants to outrage, and assault upon myself."

"Shall I place him under arrest?" asked Captain Smith recovering his wits to some degree.

"Yes," roared his lordship. Then a second later he said, "No. By thunder. No. The offences he committed were against me. It is I who will determine his sentence. See that he stands guard here all night. He is not to be relieved except on my order."

"Yes, sir," said Captain Smith.

That was only the start of the matter. That night I stood guard without relief for twelve hours. My horse was relieved, but not I. When that ordeal was over I was put on heavy stable duty, then came parade at which I had to appear spruced up to the last detail, then more stable duty.

The process was known among the men as

"flogging the rider." It was common enough when a trooper ran afoul of a non-commissioned officer. But it was almost unheard of for a commissioned officer to take this kind of revenge on a private soldier, it being considered ungentlemanly and undignified to stoop to this extent. There was even some talk, so I heard, among the officers about Lord Wedcomb's treatment of me, for the story got about. One officer, Lieutenant Greaves, who was in charge of our squadron, went so far as to say that it seemed the colonel had declared war on the men of his regiment. The remark was inspired as much by the iron discipline and the savage insistence upon attention to scruples as the treatment Lord Wedcomb subjected me to. Lieutenant Greaves was publicly reprimanded before the whole regiment. As long as Lord Wedcomb remained our commander-in-chief the lieutenant knew he could look for no promotion. And his application for a transfer was refused.

As for myself, it seemed I was court-martialed every other day for offenses so trivial I can hardly recall them. Once the under-blanket on my mount showed from beneath the saddle cloth. Although this was at the end of a day's maneuvers it was spotted by his lordship and my diet reduced to a quarter of pound of bread a day for a week with water my only liquid. It comforted me to some extent, however, that I was not the only sufferer. Lord Wedcomb set some kind of a record for courts-martial, so that Lieutenant Greaves' remark that his lordship seemed to have declared war on the Tenth Hussars was not without substance.

Actually it was war—real war, which saved me from a very foolish step. My life had been made so miserable that I determined to desert. If caught I would of course be shot. I knew this, but was prepared to take the risk. Then one day the regiment was drawn up for review and his lordship announced that Britain in alliance with France had declared war upon Russia and the Tenth Hussars had been ordered to the front.

The cheers which broke out immediately, all discipline being disregarded for the moment, must have surprised his lordship. The men of the Tenth Hussars, after months of frustration and criticism, of arduous work and nothing but abuse from their commander-in-chief, were ripe for a war with anyone, it did not matter who.

There had been rumors of conflict with Russia, but these had gone on for so long that they were given little credit. Now that it was official, that there was to be an end to the interminable drills and parades and field maneuvers and spit-and-polish living of the barracks, the enthusiasm of the men at their liberation could not be contained. They cheered and threw their caps in the air and waved their swords and since their officers joined in the display, there was nothing his lordship could do about it.

None of us knew why we were to go to war with Russia and for that matter few of us cared.

"We'll teach those Russkies not to interfere with us," Corporal Baggins, delighted at the war, said later.

"What have they done?" Peter asked him, genuinely anxious for information.

" 'Ow should I know?" demanded the corporal. "They've done something wrong otherwise we wouldn't be fighting 'em."

The corporal's attitude was that of most of the men of the regiment and, for that matter, the British expeditionary force and the whole nation.

The immediate effect of the declaration of war with Russia was that Lord Wedcomb departed for London, to consult with the War Ministry. On-the-spot command of the Tenth Hussars was given to Lieutenant Colonel Dempster, to everybody's relief, and my own persecution ceased.

Every day we expected to receive orders for overseas. But day after day we were disappointed and it began to seem that the war would certainly be over before the Tenth Hussars took the field.

Yet there were some preparations and they of an amusing nature. For one thing, a patch of leather was sewn on the seats of our tight, long-legged scarlet pants, so that they could better withstand the many hours of hard saddle wear which we all anticipated were ahead. Corporal Baggins snorted over this.

No leather reinforcement had been sewn to the seat of the pants of the Inniskilling Dragoons at Waterloo. He looked upon the move with suspicion. Again, a cutler set up shop in the barracks and sharpened all our sabres. They were normally quite dull, and several of the men cut themselves on them, trying the edge for sharpness.

Corporal Baggins did not approve of the sharpening of the sabres. "It's a long way to Moscow," he said. "They'll all be blunt by the time we get there."

Other preparations were equally futile. It was now early April and I had been some seven months in the army. Spring was here and a summer campaign promised. Yet we were given winter equipment for our horses and ourselves, it being a conviction of the higher command that since the war was against Russia and Russia was, irrespective of the season, a notoriously cold country, we should be prepared for blinding snowstorms even in August.

Finally our sailing orders came. We were to embark on a number of troopships in Dublin harbor; men, horses, and all supplies, then we would sail to join the main expeditionary force which was being collected at Plymouth, England. From there we would go through the Mediterranean, the Aegean and the Sea of Marmara to Varna in

Bulgaria where the British advance base was to be established.

Of course none but our acting commander-in-chief knew this when we went aboard. All we knew was that we were bound for the seat of the war, which Corporal Baggins believed to be around Moscow, though he had no very clear idea of the situation of Moscow. But we went very gallantly indeed through the streets of Dublin, looking brave and already triumphant in our scarlet pants, blue hussar jackets, black cloth caps; our spurs and sabres jingling and winking in the spring sunlight and the clatter of the horses' hooves on the cobbled streets making a noise at once imperative and victorious.

I believe this was the first time I actually felt proud of being a member of the Tenth Hussars. I felt almost gay, conscious of the fact that I presented an imposing figure, and began for a while to believe the common theory that we would, on meeting them, sweep the Russians before us as chaff is swept before the wind.

Matters were somewhat less impressive when we got to the docks. A petty service quarrel took place here over whether it was the duty of the navy to ferry the men and horses aboard the troopships, at anchor in mid-harbor, or whether this work should be attended to by the army. Neither, as it turned out, had made any arrangements.

It was three hours before the first lighter was

ready to take the first load of men and horses aboard. There were not sufficient lighters for the work and a task which might readily have been completed in one day, took two, with men and horses left overnight on the docks. For some reason which I cannot explain, those of us who did not get aboard the first day, were not taken back to the barracks that night.

But eventually all was done, and now began a series of trials and blunders which changed our thinking considerably about the outcome of the war. It started with our lying four days in Dublin, horses and men cramped up in the transports, waiting for a fair wind.

The horses suffered badly but there was worse ahead. We lay another week in Plymouth waiting for the rest of the expedition to get organized. And when finally we headed south to Gibraltar and turned eastwards into the Mediterranean, it was to meet the most terrible weather.

Huge seas rolled the heavy transports over on their beam ends. With each roll of the ship, the horses would be flung up against the bulwarks. They screamed and whinnied in a frenzy, threshing around, now rearing on their hind legs, now plunging down on their forelegs, uncertain of their footing, terrorized by the motion of the ship, by the half-gloom of their surroundings, and the thundering of the waves on the ship's sides.

Animals which broke a leg were crushed and

113

trampled to death by others which fell upon them. The job of quartering the horses aboard had been assigned to the navy. And the navy knew nothing of horses. They thought it sufficient to tie each animal by its head to a ring in the side of the ship. The animals were not separated from each other by stalls, so that one horse, slithering to the side, crashed into his neighbor, and an accident which should have affected but a single animal, involved a dozen.

Into this hell we of the Tenth Hussars were sent to restore some order. We tumbled down the hatch from the gun deck to find an appalling tangle of panic stricken horses below us. Nobody could give us any orders. No order could be heard above the furore. And there was no single order which could cope with such a situation.

Expecting to be kicked or crushed to death at any minute, I got over the backs of half a dozen fighting, threshing animals, thankful indeed of the lessons I'd received in horsemanship riding that brute, The Major, and found my own mount. I managed to slide down over his neck to stand to the side of him and grab him by the halter. A second later the ship rolled and my horse—a big grey called Quaker—all but crushed me to death. Obviously this was the wrong place for me to be. Indeed there was only one safe spot and that was on Quaker's back. Somehow I clambered on him, and he became quieter immediately.

It is a remarkable thing about a cavalry horse, but he feels lost in strange circumstances unless he has his rider on his back. Then, however strange the circumstances, he gains a measure of confidence. Certainly Quaker became calmer and looking about quickly I saw most of the men of the Hussars had got on the backs of their chargers so that some of the whinneying and rearing about died down.

But obviously we couldn't remain mounted on our horses through the long voyage to Bulgaria. The next thing to be done was to rig some kind of stall to separate the animals, and on this work we spent a good sixty hours. The weather continued vile for all that time. Ten horses had broken legs and had to be got out of the hold, destroyed and dumped overboard. Later in the voyage we didn't dump the dead horses. We turned them over to the ship's crew, who butchered them and salted down much of the meat, and declared it infinitely superior to the pickled "beef" (mostly horse anyway) with which her Majesty's ships were provided.

In the whole voyage there was hardly a week of good weather, and when we arrived at Varna, our port of debarkation, more than half our mounts were sick. I dwell upon the horses but naturally the men suffered too. There were broken collar bones aplenty, and not a man aboard below the rank of commissioned officer whose face was not swollen and bloodied from the struggles with the animals below. We were a very different body of men from the brightly uniformed hussars who had ridden so proudly through the streets of Dublin.

And yet we never for one moment doubted that once ashore, whatever Russian forces were sent against us, we would scatter with the greatest ease. Even Corporal Baggins, despite the blunders of the voyage and the ineptitude of our officers, was of the opinion that the Russians would be no match for the British cavalry. As for my friend Peter Storey, who was nursing a sprained wrist as a result of his struggles with his mount aboard the troopship, he said, "Without a doubt we will defeat the Russians—that is if the navy and our own officers don't defeat us first."

CHAPTER THIRTEEN

LORD WEDCOMB HAD NOT ACCOMPANIED the regiment to Varna but had gone to the seat of war (or what we supposed was to be the seat of war) on his private yacht, the Neptune, arriving a week after we disembarked. With him came his sister, Lady Barbara, on whose horse I had made my escape, years ago, it seemed, in Galway. For the time being, at least, his lordship had forgotten about me. He had a war on his hands, and so I was spared his personal persecution.

It now being early summer, we were stationed in a place which the native peoples avoided during the hot months because it was full of cholera. Within a few days of our landing, there were several cases of cholera reported in our camp. Added to this the horses were in far worse condition than had been supposed. More than one-third of them would never be of any use for active campaigning. They could be ridden only lightly, and for short intervals. After the cholera outbreak we moved camp to a place several miles inland. This did no good, for Lord Wedcomb

refused to consult the natives about local condition, holding them filthy, barbarous and ignorant
and in no position to advise a British nobleman,
particularly a British colonel of cavalry. The place
we moved to was empty of houses of any kind.
There was a good spring and plenty of grass. But
it never struck his lordship that there might be a
good reason why so pleasant a valley should be so
deserted. The reason was that the valley was
called by the Bulgarians "The Valley of Death."
It was full of cholera. I believe the ground itself
was infected with the disease and the water from
the spring saturated with it.

Men were stricken right and left. They would
lie down comfortably to sleep at night only to
awaken in terrible pain, spend an hour or two
vomiting and sweating with agony, and then, in
many cases, die. Peter Storey was one of the first
to get the plague. I did what I could for him—
indeed I had to even if he were not my friend.
There was no army nursing service. A soldier who
became sick was to be tended by his comrades who
were not engaged upon any other duty. Other
duty, of course, came first. But I stuck with Peter,
giving him boiled water when he needed it, and
moving him constantly, for he would be seized
with fits of uncontrollable nausea and empty the
contents of his stomach where he lay, being too
weak to do anything for himself.

I knew nothing at all of how to treat Peter, but

one of the natives, who had attached himself (at great risk) to our camp as a kind of general servant, brought a fine clay mixed to a cloudy consistency in water, and told me by sign language that Peter should drink this. I made him do so, and whether it was the clay that did it or some other factor I do not know, but Peter recovered after a week, though many others died.

The reason there was nothing for us to do at our camp in Bulgaria was that the Russians were not to be found. They had originally invaded the country, but before our arrival had withdrawn, though how far we did not know. To ascertain where the Russians were, Lord Wedcomb decided to lead a reconnaissance of a hundred men in the direction of the Danube, which marked the boundary of Russia and Bulgaria. Lady Barbara, his sister, decided that she must by all means join this reconnaissance and it was my fortune to be one of the men picked for the expedition, largely, I believe, because I was one of the few fit for the journey, having escaped sickness so far.

Lady Barbara was a very high-spirited girl— dark haired, her face as soft and white as milk and her eyes deep brown. She was reckoned a great beauty and something of a madcap, and looked upon the war with Russia as a great lark in which she intended to share. When she learned that her brother was to lead a reconnaissance to seek the enemy she determined to ride with him, and Lord Wedcomb gave way. His sister was the one person in the world who had any real control over him.

We set out at dawn and rode all day under a blazing sun with but brief pauses to rest, and without catching a sight of the enemy. The heat was intense. Swarms of grasshoppers flew in clouds out of the long grass as we pushed through it, making a shrill noise which drowned out the jingling of our equipment. The country was wonderful riding terrain—perfect for cavalry work and Lord Wedcomb set a hot pace.

The following day was the same and went without incident. But on the third day, when we were within sight of the Danube River, still without a trace of the enemy, his lordship decided that it would be a brilliant maneuver to cover several miles during the night. A brilliant maneuver it would have been too, had we known anything of the country through which we were riding. But we had not even a map of the place. And to add to the hazard of getting lost, his lordship decided to split the scouting party up into two groups. One was to go up the river for two hours and then return. The other was to go down the river for the same period and come back.

He led one group and Lady Barbara decided she would go with the other. Naturally I contrived to be with the men under the command of Lieutenant Greaves, who, in turn, was part of Lady

Barbara's group. I did not want to be one of fifty horsemen under the command of my arch enemy Lord Wedcomb.

We had ridden no more than an hour when we came upon a thick wood. Lieutenant Greaves decided to go through this, though it would have been far better to have skirted it. It was inevitable that his small force, choosing game paths through the wood, should become separated, and as luck would have it, I found myself trailing behind Lady Barbara. We were two horsemen very close to enemy territory and with no clear idea where the rest of our group was. It did not dawn upon either of us for some time that we had become separated from the main body. I was merely following the horseman ahead, not knowing that the rider was Lady Barbara. She, however, in her independent way, instead of following the man in front of her, elected to take another path and so we became lost.

She halted in a clearing and waited for me to come up to her. It was only then that I discovered who she was.

"We're lost," she said. "Isn't it thrilling?"

"My Lady," I replied, "we had better move to our left. The river is in that direction and if we follow it, we must come upon the others."

"I propose to do nothing of the kind," she snapped. "I am going straight ahead and I order you to follow me."

"I must rejoin the main group," I replied. "I cannot take orders from you."

"Very well," she said. "Go your own way. I shall go mine." She urged her horse forward down a path which would take her obliquely away from the river and therefore from the rest of the men. It was just willfulness that made her do this and I was in a quandary. I could not leave her. And yet I could not deliberately ride away from where I suspected the rest of our force was.

I caught up with her and pleaded that she should return with me in the direction of the river. She refused. Then she recognized me for the first time.

"Aren't you the Galway boy who beat my brother?" she asked.

"Yes," I replied.

"I gave you my horse to save your life," she said. "But you deserved to be whipped for beating my brother. How did you dare raise a hand to your superiors?"

To this I made no reply, more out of anger than discretion, for I boiled at the thought that she held her brother superior to me and myself some kind of serf or slave.

"You had better come with me, Lady Barbara," I said, between clenched teeth.

"I will do nothing of the sort," she replied.

"Very well, then," I said, "you leave me no choice." Reaching down I seized the bridle of her horse, jerked the reins from her hands, and moved off towards the river, leading her horse behind me. She struck at me several times with her riding whip, but without much success. Then she fell to swearing, quite prettily, though it was shocking to hear a girl use such language. Then she started pleading, or perhaps coaxing would be the better word. But it was all to no avail. I would not let her have the reins back, and all she could do, if she wished to be parted from me, was dismount and remain alone in the forests on the banks of the Danube.

We had not gone for more than twenty minutes or so when the trees started to thin out and we were once more upon open ground. About a hundred yards away, I could see the silver streak of the Danube, a very wide river at this point. But there was still no sign of the rest of our force. I let Lady Barbara have her reins back and she took them in silence.

I was just about to suggest that we go back up the river when two or three small mounted figures moved between us and the silver water. Lady Barbara immediately cried out to them, and spurring her horse, set out in a canter. I followed her, surprised and cursing her for her foolishness for the horsemen might be Russians as readily as they might be our own.

It turned out that they were Russians. I caught the outline of one of them, dark against the bright surface of the river, and realized that he was not wearing the uniform of the hussars.

"Back," I shouted to Lady Barbara. "Turn back." She reined in, hesitated for a moment, and then turned. "Make for the wood," I cried and drew my sabre.

There were three of the Russians, armed with lances, and they must have recognized us as enemies immediately. One lowered his lance and started riding at a diagonal, made for Lady Barbara. He, I knew, was the man to be dealt with at once and I had the advantage of perhaps fifty feet less ground to cover than he before he reached his quarry.

Lady Barbara fled past me and I had a glimpse of her white face with her hair flying in the wind as she went by. The next thing I saw was the bulk of the Russian's horse and his lance-head gleaming in the starlight. Sabre against lance is no match, for the swordsman is at a tremendous disadvantage due to the length of the lance. But there was no help for it. There was but one thing to do and I did it. I flung myself quickly over one side of Quaker, crouching against his flank away from the Russian. It was done in a second and the Russian had not a chance to alter his point of aim. The lance swept within inches of my mount and had I remained in the saddle, I would have been skewered like a rabbit. Then I pulled Quaker's head around and remounting properly, swept down on the Russian from behind. He had not yet recovered from the speed of his charge, and I caught him as he was turning his horse. I felt a shock as the point of my sabre took him in the throat and then I was on galloping for the wood. His two comrades stopped when they got to him, and I managed to make the woods safely enough. Lady Barbara I found a few hundred feet inside.

"Come on," I shouted. "As fast as you can." But there was no further pursuit. The Russians must have concluded that there were several British cavalry scouts in the wood and they were outnumbered and so we got safely away.

"Did you kill him?" Lady Barbara asked when there was time for questions.

"I believe so," I replied.

"You saved my life," she said.

"Why then," I replied, "we are even. For you saved mine once."

"It is strange," she continued, "that because I took pity on an Irish tenant on the banks of the Shannon my life should be saved on the banks of the Danube."

"As for that," I said, with some heat, "though you find it hard to believe, Irish tenants are men like other men, and I only did what any man in the same circumstances would have done."

"If I were my brother," she said, ignoring my anger, "would you have saved me?"

"Your brother's a man—or at least he's a male," I said. "He could fend for himself."

"But would you have saved me at the risk of your own life?" she asked.

"No," I said. "I wouldn't have. I owe your brother nothing but hatred."

"You should love your enemies," she said.

"There is an equal duty on my enemies to love me," I replied. The rest of the journey, until we caught up with some troopers sent by Lieutenant Greaves to scour the woods for us, was passed in silence.

I was sorry I had replied so angrily and with so much venom to Lady Barbara's questions, but was too proud to say so. And I was worried about the effect on my future should she repeat our conversation to her brother.

CHAPTER FOURTEEN

LORD WEDCOMB'S RECONNAISSANCE established the fact that the Russians had definitely withdrawn from Bulgaria and were now back in their own country. This meant that the British expeditionary force, or at least the part of the force which we of the Tenth Hussars and the other cavalry units represented, were in the wrong place and indeed the wrong country. And it became obvious as the days went by that the longer we stayed there the worse it would be for us, for the cholera epidemic showed no signs of abating. Furthermore, our horses suffered from grass sickness and hoof fever. We had arrived expecting to live off the country, to find plenty of forage for the animals and food for the men. We found forage but not food for the troops who were in the poorest way. As things stood, the Russians had to do nothing to defeat us. They had merely to hope that we would remain in the cholera country which they had forsaken, and we would defeat ourselves.

This fact gradually became apparent to the high command. And the high command decided that with an army half of which was incapacitated

by illness, an army for which there were few pro-
visions, and for which no reliable arrangements
had been made to obtain provision from England,
we must invade Russia. The invasion would be
made through that southern peninsula of Russia
which thrust into the Black Sea and was called the
Crimea.

So we embarked on the troopships once more
and once more went through the ordeal, lasting
several days, of tending our hysterical horses,
many of them now desperately weak, until at last
we landed on the Crimean coast at a place called
Eupatoria. There we rested long enough to bury
our dead—there were a number of them—and
arrange for those too sick to accompany the army
to be taken on transports back to England.

Then, with no maps of the country, no knowledge of the lay of the land as far as a few miles
ahead, with no baggage trains to amount to anything, no idea of where the next drinkable water
supply was to be found, and no information of the
strength or location of the enemy, we set out to
invade Russia.

There was a good deal of grumbling among the
men about this state of affairs. They said loudly
enough for their officers to hear that they had
come to fight and not to die of disease. And their
officers could only pretend they did not hear. They
themselves were discontented, seeing their squadrons reduced and the whole campaign, which

they hoped would bring them glory and promotion, horribly bungled.

Only Corporal Baggins remained unmoved. He had not contracted cholera, and had an invariable formula to settle all doubts. "We don't know nothing and we don't have to know nothing," he would say. "Just carry out orders. That's all you've got to do and let the officers do the worrying."

Yet I believe he was dimly worried himself. Certainly the state of the British army was far from that which existed when the great Wellington was the commander-in-chief and every soldier could be sure of a regular supply of water and rations, powder and shot.

Of Lady Barbara I saw nothing after our adventure on the banks of the Danube. Whether she told her brother about it and of our conversation, I did not know. Lord Wedcomb seemed to have forgotten all about me, and for that I was grateful. He and Lady Barbara sailed on their yacht from Varna to Calamita Bay off the Crimean coast near where we landed.

Our first day's march from Eupatoria across a sunlit undulating grassy country alive with wild game brought joy among the ranks. The joy resulted from the fact that the men felt that at last they were going somewhere, that there was a specific objective ahead, and a job to be done. The men felt that the long weeks of waiting around in a camp where death struck down their comrades by the hour was over. They cheered when a bird flew up out of the grass by the column, and they gave hunting shouts as hares broke cover and ran bounding, their ears upright, away to right or left.

But the cholera marched with us. As the day went on, and the sun continued to blaze without mercy from an impersonal and unending sky, more and more men dropped behind. Some fell writhing to the ground and were joined by one or two of their comrades trying to help them. Four hours of march and we seemed like an army retreating from defeat in battle rather than advancing to the conflict. The column of infantry straggled over two miles or more. Their track was marked with a litter of equipment. Many men struggled along supported on the arms of their fellows.

And then we caught our first glimpse of the Russian Cossacks. They appeared, a fringe of splendidly mounted men, on the hills to the right and left of us. The air was so clear we could see the details of their uniforms clearly—the crossed cartridge belts, the hats of fur, and loose trousers which contrasted with our own tight garments. They made no attempt to attack. They just watched us through telescopes and then hurriedly moved off.

Lieutenant Greaves, in charge of our squadron, asked permission to charge one body of the Russian horse. Permission was refused. The fact was that the cavalry had become seriously weakened. We were to be held out of action as long as possible, and only allowed to engage the enemy if the need was desperate.

All through the afternoon we were under the constant watch of bodies of Cossacks who could not have failed to note the weakened condition of the army and the amount of equipment which we left behind. That evening we came to a small river, the Bulganek. It lay at the bottom of a deep though gentle valley. On the slopes opposite we saw large bodies of Cossacks and Russian dragoons. One group of cavalry went out to reconnoiter towards them. But they were brought back without action. The men took this badly, for the Russians jeered at them as they retreated.

That night we camped by the river, expecting that we would have a battle on our hands the following day. The opposite slopes of the valley were pricked with the camp fires of the Russians. The horizon was lit spasmodically by farm houses to which the Cossacks set fire so that we would not take over any food in the barns. Haystacks burned brilliantly around us. We were to live off the country—but the enemy was destroying the country's food supply.

The following day, to our surprise, the enemy had gone. Some thought that they were afraid and anxious to avoid an engagement. I found this hard to believe, and suspected that we were being led into a trap. Peter was unworried. He had now quite recovered from the cholera and was deeply grateful to me for looking after him. He contrived to be with me at all times and I knew that if we ever did get into battle, he would be at my side wherever I went.

"When we attack, or are attacked, it will be time enough to worry," he said. "Meanwhile, I'm going to fill my canteen."

Corporal Baggins repeated his old philosophy. We had just to carry out orders and all would be well.

We did meet the enemy that day though. We met them on their grounds, on their terms, in masses sufficient to have overwhelmed us all. And to our astonishment we defeated them.

The place of the battle was on the opposite bank of a river six miles or so further on. The river was called the Alma, and we reached it about noon. It came dramatically into view. We topped the crown of a long hill and there at the bottom of a gentle grassy slope was the swift flowing stream. But the bank opposite us upon which the enemy was drawn up for battle was a natural citadel, which it seemed quite impossible to take.

This opposite bank was not a grassy slope. At the river's edge there was a fifteen foot cliff to be scaled. Beyond that was a stone-covered steep slope, the stones as gray as armor in the sunlight.

At the top of this was a flat area bristling with Russian guns. From their position the Russians could fire upon us all the way down our bank of the river, continue pouring bullets, grape shot, roundshot, and shrapnel into us as we crossed the river, and maintain this murderous fire as we tried to scramble up the stone-strewn slope. And the final assault would be into a veritable hedge of Russian muskets.

There was one other natural fortification in the hands of the Russians. This consisted of a hill cropping out of the stone slope on which two Russian batteries had been placed. The lower was a big battery with support from a smaller one above. The two batteries could command the slope and it was plain that they would have to be taken first.

When I saw all this I experienced a mixture of both anger and fear. The fear was natural enough. The anger arose out of the utter stupidity of our commanders who had led us forward, without any attempt at scouting, to a place where we could all be slaughtered by the enemy at will. They had first bundled us unprepared into troopships to wrestle horses for which no stabling arrangements had been made, they had landed us in a country infested with cholera and kept us there week after week, and now they led us into a position where we would all be slaughtered or taken prisoner. And all this they did because they had the right to do it as noblemen with money sufficient to buy a high command in the army. Rank and money entitled them to sacrifice their fellow countrymen and call it glory.

Lord Wedcomb sat a hundred feet from me on his horse, the symbol of all this privileged bungling, and my hatred of him rose at that moment to a peak it never achieved before.

This flush of fear and anger was followed immediately by a sense of terrible foreboding. I became quite certain that in some way I was chained to Lord Wedcomb and must follow him without escape until he had finally brought about my death. The feeling came strongly to me that this man was to be the agent of my doom. This conviction never left me in the weeks that followed. Lord Wedcomb became for me the enemy —not the Russians—and only if he died first could I hope to live.

Our battle plan, confronted with such a terrible situation, was very simple. The infantry were deployed in two lines over an area covering nearly two miles. They dressed, man upon man, company on company, with parade ground precision and snap. We, of the cavalry, numbering in all about a thousand horse, were drawn up in squadrons on the extreme left of the infantry, whose right flank was guarded by the ocean. When the two long lines had dressed, the bugles sounded the advance, the drummer boys of each regiment waved their sticks in a flourish in the air, the fifers squealed into a march, and the two red lines keeping perfect formation, started down the grassy slope towards the river.

It was an astonishing spectacle. The two ranks stepped off in perfect unison and started down the slope without the slightest hesitation. And then the Russian gunners opened fire and the bank opposite blazed with gun flashes and smoke. Gaps were torn in the two lines of soldiers but they continued on, never increasing their pace, never diminishing it, merely closing up to fill the vacant spaces.

The bottom of the valley soon became thick with smoke. The enemy had set fire to a small hamlet which lay on their side of the river and billows of smoke rolled out from this so that the red-coated British lines disappeared from our view. After a while the lines reappeared. The men had crossed the river and now struggled up the stone slope toward the Russian positions and particularly towards the two batteries on the hill. They still maintained their parade ground formation.

We of the cavalry had not moved. Our orders were to remain where we were. We had a bird's eye view of the whole action and could see the small red puppets climbing up the slope, numbers of them dropping but the remainder going forward coolly and unhurried.

The men went into a hail of fire of every kind from musket to heavy cannon, closer and closer to the two batteries.

Then, when they were within a hundred feet of the batteries, the nerve of the Russian gunners broke. They fled from their positions in the heavy battery and, with a cheer which we could hear plainly, the British charged and took possession of the guns.

But they were hardly in occupation before a huge mass of Russian infantry started down the slope towards them. I could not say what the odds were—fifty to one would be perhaps a fair guess. Our men were driven out of the battery and the two red lines pushed, before this enormous weight of infantry, backward to the river.

By now, however, two reserve lines of infantry had been formed upon our bank of the river. They consisted of the Guards regiment and the Scottish Highlanders. These went down the bank and crossed the river as the red-coated infantry had done before. They went in the same parade order, climbed the opposite bank and once again a huge mass of Russian infantry appeared. They came in a horde that darkened the ground opposite. It seemed that every foot soldier in Russia came pouring down upon the two lines of Guards and Highlanders, through which the redcoated soldiers, sent into action first, had managed to drift to reform their ranks.

It would seem inevitable that the line of the Guards and Highlanders must be cut in two by this massive battering ram of Russian infantry and the day turned into a rout. But nothing of the sort happened. The British lines merely surrounded the Russian column and we could hear the crack of their Minie guns as they fired into the enemy. The effect was like an army of bright ants attacking some huge gray beast. The Russians were so closely packed that a great majority of them could not use their weapons. The big Russian column stopped and seemed to shudder. And then the Russians broke and fled in blocks and tatters of lines back up their bank of the valley.

Now was the time for a cavalry charge, to run them down while they were demoralized. I saw Lord Wedcomb arguing with a staff officer but could not hear what was said above the noise of the battle. The trumpeter sounded a charge, and we urged our horses over into the valley across the stream and went scrambling up the banks.

This was my first taste of action. The brush with the Cossacks on the banks of the Danube had been in the nature of a duel. This was battle. In five minutes we were upon the Russians, who had now gained the heights atop the valley, sabering them and riding them down. We could have chased them I believe as far as Sebastopol and broken their army completely. And then, at the peak of the pursuit, with every chance to capture many of the Russian guns, the trumpet sounded the retreat.

What might have been an overwhelming victory was thus converted into merely a local victory. The British commander-in-chief, I learned later, was outraged that the cavalry had charged without his direct orders. He had taken up a position where he could hardly see the whole field and did not know the situation. But he had one overwhelming desire—and that was to save his cavalry.

We were ordered back and back we went, freeing what prisoners we had taken. The river Alma had been crossed. The Russian positions were in our hands. But the Russian army, still intact, still with its guns, was able to retreat to Sebastopol. The blunders of the war were continuing.

As we sat around our campfires that night and discussed our utterly stupid recall, Peter summed up the feelings of the men of the Tenth Hussars. "The high command," he said, "is without a doubt at this moment thinking up some blunder so great that it will go down in history and make them famous for centuries to come. But all we have to do is carry out their orders and everything will be fine. That right, Corporal?"

Corporal Baggins was too disgruntled to reply. He didn't say so but we knew what he was thinking—namely that Wellington would never have handled matters in that fashion at Waterloo.

CHAPTER FIFTEEN

A MONTH LATER THE BIG BLUNDER of which Peter had spoken jokingly was made. In the interval, the Russians had withdrawn to Sebastopol, and we stayed some time at Alma, burying our dead and giving the enemy every opportunity to reinforce the defenses of the city. It was now generally known that our objective was to take Sebastopol, and the fleet was sent around to the harbor near that city. We went by land, making a terrible journey of it, for again we had no maps of the territory, and blundered through woods and thickets which we might have gone around had we known anything of the territory.

Lord Wedcomb was as angry as a hornet at being recalled from the charge at Alma. Indeed everybody in the cavalry was angry over the order, and when, after encircling Sebastopol it became known that we were to besiege the city, it was the consensus that we might as well all be back in England. Cavalry are useless in a siege. We could see ourselves waiting in muddy tents with half starved horses through a long winter of wind and rain and without any active duty to perform.

Matters fell out very differently, however. The Russians had no intention of leaving us sitting outside their city with our headquarters in a village called Balaclava. As the days went by stories were brought in by the Crimean peasants of a large Russian army moving towards us. They were discounted.

Then the Turks, who formed a portion of our army with the French, reported a big Russian detachment getting ready for attack. This proved to be a false report. However, the evidence of the massing of a big Russian force could no longer be disputed. They appeared on the hills to the north of us and set up guns overlooking our position. These hills were called the Fedioukine Heights. The Russian batteries there could command our position. But facing these heights, and with a roadway from the village of Balaclava, was another range which was in our hands. We had our batteries of guns on them, and they were manned by the Turks. So everything was thought safe enough.

Then came the final blow. The Russians, early on the morning of October 25, launched an attack upon our Turkish guns, which were lightly manned. Before reinforcements could be brought up the guns had been taken. Now the Russians had guns on both lines of hills, and furthermore had captured the road which led to our base at Balaclava. That road was the only supply road for our army and vital to us.

All that morning a kind of disorganized fighting took place. It was impossible for the men in the Tenth Hussars, forming a unit of what was known as the Light Brigade, to know what was going on. We could hear the noise of the battle. We could see smoke rolling in clouds from the horizon. But there was not an enemy in sight of us. The countryside around consisted of a series of little hills, not much more than twenty or thirty feet high, like ocean rollers. Somewhere in these hills or beyond them a battle was raging. But of it we could see nothing.

This was the situation in the Light Brigade for the whole of that forenoon. We stood to horse, ready to go into action, utterly uncertain of what was taking place, of whether a major attack by the whole Russian force had been launched, of whether the enemy was in front of us, to the side of us, or behind us. All we knew was that we had no orders to do anything but remain where we were. The men were nearly beside themselves with vexation and frustration, and Lord Wedcomb, at the head of his regiment, kept riding his charger nervously up and down, and then going off to consult with the other regimental commanders.

Finally he came back, his face flushed with excitement. "We are to charge the guns," he shouted to Captain Smith, his aide. "Fall in upon the Eighth Hussars to the left."

"What guns?" said Peter to nobody in particular.

The question stirred Corporal Baggins out of his usual unquestioning acceptance of any military order. "Them guns the Russians took from the Turks, of course," he said. And this was what everybody believed as we formed up in line.

The area where we assembled was between the two ranges of hills of which I have already spoken, that is to say the Fedioukine Heights on our left and the line of hills on our right upon which the Turkish guns, newly captured by the Russians, lay. Between these two lines of hills was a valley about a mile long, with at the end of it the major body of the Russian army, deployed behind a further line of guns which blocked the end of the valley.

When we came into view of this valley, flanked by a line of guns on either side, and sealed by further guns at the far end, there was a remarkable occurrence. By some freak of the wind, a great cloud of smoke or perhaps it was fog rolled in, so that the valley floor disappeared from view, leaving only the top of the hills to right and left visible. This mist remained in position for perhaps five minutes and then slowly drifted away.

The phenomenon had a deep effect upon me. I recalled in a flash, out of the limbo of my memory, that Tom of the Three Fingers had said that such a mist always appeared shortly before the

142

reappearance of the strange jewel, the Foggy Dew. I had long forgotten his story, for so many things had happened to me since the day he told it. Now the details of the legend concerning the strange opal came clearly and swiftly to my mind. Whoever found it was to go through a period of great trial and ordeal. Then a mysterious mist would appear. And then the Foggy Dew would be found.

I tried to rid my mind of this nonsense, as I called it, recalling that Tom of the Three Fingers was but a rogue and had probably made the tale up. But the impression and recollection were too strong. As we wheeled our horses into line for the charge I was still thinking about the legend of the stone, the thought so strong that it drove out any fear or apprehension which I might have had as we prepared to grapple with the enemy.

"Are you all right?" Peter asked, looking queerly at me.

"Yes," I replied. "Why?"

"You look strange. White," he said.

"It's that mist that gave me a turn, appearing so suddenly," I replied.

"Hanged if I ever will understand you," Peter said, shaking his head. "Here we are about to charge the guns, and you're talking about the weather."

"Silence in the ranks," roared Corporal Baggins, and that put an end to our exchange.

This line for the charge, in which we were now

drawn up, gave the place of honor to the Tenth Hussars, the Thirteenth Light Dragoons, and the Seventeenth Lancers. We formed the first of three rows of cavalry. Our regimental commanders rode ahead of each regiment, his officers after him, and then the troopers. Out in front was Lord Cardigan, Commander of the Light Brigade, an elderly man noted more for his temper than his brains. It was common talk among us that there was more brains in his lordship's horse than in his lordship's head.

On my right was Peter and on my left Corporal Baggins, solid as a block of cement. There was some kind of conference with Lord Cardigan, and then his lordship raised his sword and his words came clearly back to us. "The brigade will advance," he said. "Walk. March. Trot"—these being the speeds to be assumed during the charge. One lone trumpet shrilled, and then, in a strange silence, uninterrupted by the report of a single gun, we moved slowly forward into the valley.

It struck me that the silence was as if the world was holding its breath. It lasted perhaps for no more than a few seconds. It was broken by only minor, commonplace sounds which on the eve of battle had a certain unreality to them. I recall the tinkle of bits and spurs, the muffled thud of the horses' hooves upon the short thick grass and the sudden shrilling of a chorus of crickets. The creaking of my stirrup leathers was clearly audible to me and Peter's mount, snorting loudly and shaking its head with impatience, gave me a start.

Then the guns spoke. The air was shaken by their thunder. The horses started nervously and the hills on both sides blossomed white with gunsmoke. From that moment silence was utterly destroyed. It seemed that the world had had its last spell of quiet and from then forward there would be nothing but the thunder of guns, the high whine of cannister and grape flinging through the air, the dull moan of roundshot and the sharp fiery explosion of shells.

A lieutenant, riding directly ahead of me, was the first man I saw fall. One second he was sitting straight and easy in his saddle, the next his horse had pivoted around and the whole side of the officer's face was a mass of blood and bone. He raised his sword and stood up in his stirrups and then plummeted to the ground. His horse hesitated and then, obedient to its long training, moved on ahead of us, riderless and nervous.

We were now in such a position that we should wheel to the right and charge the Turkish guns. I saw an officer dash out of the ranks to Lord Cardigan and point to the Turkish battery. Cardigan waved him back and a second later the officer was dead, decapitated by the roundshot. Whatever had been his message it had not been delivered. It became plain that we were not to charge the Turkish battery on our right. Instead we were to attack the Russian guns at the end of the valley. To do this we would have to ride down between the two enemy batteries on the hills on either side, caught in heavy fire from right, left, and from dead ahead. Someone had made a mistake, another of the blunders which had marked the whole war to date. We were to pay for it.

I became convinced that I was to die that day. The invisible chain of doom which bound me to Lord Wedcomb, riding ahead of me, had led me here. It was his mission in life to see that I was killed and he was performing it. There was no escape.

We were still moving at a parade ground walk, advancing between the cross-fire of two batteries of cannon and into the frontal fire of a third. But the pace did not change. The air was thick with shot now. Men were flung by invisible hands from their horses to fall in butchered heaps upon the ground. Sometimes they cried out. Sometimes they died without a sound. I glanced to my left. The line was still perfectly dressed, not one man permitted his mount to get ahead of the rest. But there were gaps in the line where cannon shot had plowed through in volleys like a sickle through standing corn.

"Close up! Close on the center," Lieutenant Greaves shouted. The men closed in to fill the gaps, and riding boot to boot presented a more compact target for the guns. The guns never stopped. They roared from every side and their thick white smoke slid slowly down the hills towards us. The ground below us seemed in torment. It writhed, jerked, spouted upward, and shook under the cannonade. Patches of grass caught fire. Clods of turf were flung up by shell explosions. The earth was no longer a quiet thing, but a heaving surface which seemed itself to be exploding.

"Close up. Close up. Dress on the center." We closed up again. I glanced behind. A line of what had once been two hundred horsemen was reduced to a little more than a hundred. Packs of riderless horses were milling and galloping around. I caught one swift glance of the part of the valley we had come over. It was strewn with men and horses, dead and dying. The batteries were still firing into them.

Still we went on, and still at a walk. I expected death at every second, and having expected it now for fully five minutes I no longer cared. I would die. But scores of others were dying, as good men as me. It did not matter.

When we were halfway down the valley Corporal Baggins fell. I heard him swear loudly and turning saw that his uniform was drenched with blood. He slumped forward across his charger's neck and then, quite slowly, slipped to the ground. It was the kind of end he would have wished for— the only fitting end for him. Life had come to its fruition in one cavalry charge. It came to its conclusion in another.

Now I sat alone and on either side of me were several riderless horses, many of them badly wounded and bleeding copiously. The poor brutes were in a state of near panic. Their huge eyes were red, their flanks covered with sweat and blood. Yet they kept to the line obedient to their training. The two nearest me on either side crowded close seeking the comfort of a rider, and I had to beat at them with my sabre to avoid my legs being crushed. The smoke in the valley was now so thick that I could scarcely see the officers ahead. The thunder of the guns continued. We were within easy range of the Russian heavy batteries at the end of the valley, and they shelled us unmercifully. Sheets of flame and smoke rolled up from the earth. It was as if we were going through a fiery pit. And still the order was to walk.

It was at this point that I recalled the dream which I had had the night that Tom of the Three Fingers had told me of the Foggy Dew. The dream had been of a number of skeleton figures flashing by on horses, and set in the head of each horse was a gleaming jewel.

The recollection came in a flash. I looked around. Surely this was the dream come true. Surely the men I could see to right and left, over the backs of riderless horses were dead. And the bright headstrap decorations on the horses themselves—were they not jewels? The fancy mounted almost to conviction, for I was nearly hysterical at the slaughter around—a slaughter too horrible to describe. It is one thing to see a horse dead of a wound. It is another to see a horse, its chest and sides ripped open so as to expose the bone, walking along beside you, covered with blood and seeking to nuzzle you with gory nostrils. Certainly everybody was dead, the horses as well as the men. And I was the only living soul in a nightmare charge of corpses.

Lord Wedcomb rode ahead of me, visible through the battle smoke only from the waist up. He was dead too I thought and I laughed when this occurred to me.

From somewhere to the right and front a bugle now sounded the full charge. The thunder of the guns had increased so that I knew we must be very nearly upon them. The line of horses to either side, with only an occasional rider to be seen, increased its pace. We broke from a walk to a trot, from a trot to a canter, from a canter to a gallop. Through the smoke ahead I could now see jets of flame, orange and deep red. Lord Wedcomb appeared for a moment outlined in a halo of flame. I rose in my stirrups, sabre held high and in five paces was among the Russian guns. A gray figure rose before me with a rammer in his hands. He went reeling back from my sabre cut. I saw another kneeling, his rifle pointed at me, and jerked

149

Quaker up on his haunches. The poor animal took the shot in his belly and crumbled screaming to the ground.

What happened next has no continuity for me. I recall struggling to get my feet out of my stirrups and a horse and rider sailed over my head. Something struck me heavily at the base of the neck, but I got up, and seeing a riderless charger standing quietly between two guns, I leaped on his back and beat him forward with the flat of my sword. Then I was out of the gunsmoke and out of the guns. There was a little clearing with five or six of our Hussars lining up in it. I rode over and joined them, and when I got there saw that Wedcomb was one of their number.

"You're not dead?" I shouted at him.

"Nor you?" he asked.

In that moment a number of Russian dragoons appeared out of the smoke to the right of us, coming forward in column. They were, I am sure, as astonished to see us as we to see them. They stood stock still for a few seconds and then, at a curt order, a group of perhaps ten detached themselves from the main body and bore down upon us. We met them horse to horse, savage in our fury, hacking and thrusting, careless of hurt to ourselves. We were through them in less time than it takes to relate.

Wheeling I saw Wedcomb unhorsed, and limping towards me. We were alone in an area, cut off

150

from our fellows by billows of gunsmoke. Safety now depended on getting back through the line of Russian guns which we had charged and up that terrible valley again.

"Trooper," Wedcomb shouted at me. "Give me a stirrup." He was within six feet of me. I now had my chance to kill him. I could ride him down, sabre him, or leave him to the Russian dragoons to deal with. He reached out a hand and at that moment recognized me.

"You," he shouted, and I could see he expected death.

"Jump," I yelled, not knowing why, and leaning down caught him around the armpits and pulled him across the front of my saddle. Then a Russian Cossack appeared in my path out of the smoke. I was holding Wedcomb with one hand and struck at the Cossack with my sabre with the other. It was a wild blow and quite useless. There was a blinding flash right before my eyes and I was jerked back off the horse. Wedcomb grabbed for me ineffectually and then disappeared into the smoke around the guns.

CHAPTER SIXTEEN

FOR WHAT SEEMED quite some time I lay on the ground fully conscious and unconcerned about what was going to happen to me. I could feel no pain and could not understand how I had come to fall from my horse. I believed I was going to die, and that Wedcomb had been the agent of my death as I had expected. Then I tried to roll over, for I had fallen on my side, but could not get any leverage from my left arm. It lay under my body, but it might as well have been somebody else's limb for all the control I had over it.

I pushed myself up with my right arm and so got into a sitting position. The whole of my tunic was covered with blood. But this had no special meaning for me. I looked at it dully and wondered whose it could be. Then two men appeared before me. They were Russians. One of them said something and smiled from behind a huge mustache.

I just looked at him, for I did not know what he meant. Between the two of them they raised me to my feet, and then put me across the back of a horse. The horse started walking away and I lost consciousness.

When I regained my senses I was in a large room propped against a wall. My hussar tunic had been taken off and my arm was strapped to my side and bandaged. There were also some heavy bandages around my neck, but I could move my right arm. I still had on the rest of my uniform, so I knew I had not been unconscious long.

There were three other British cavalrymen in the room, which I took to be part of a hospital. Among them was Peter Storey.

"Peter!" I cried. "How did you manage to get here? I saw you go down and thought you were dead."

"It was only the horse," said Peter. "I got another mount and came along in the third line."

"Where are you hurt?" I asked, for I could see no sign of bandaging on him.

"I'm not," he said. "I'm just a prisoner. There's four of us here altogether. I got cut off and was captured."

The other two men were in a very bad way. One had his whole left leg in thick bandages and dark patches of blood had already appeared on the outside. Another slumped deathly white in a corner. He was missing a forearm, and his face had the sheen of wax. Two Russian doctors were busy with these men.

"I didn't think I'd come through that alive," I said.

A Russian dressed in a splendid uniform now came through a door at one end of the room. His pantaloons were wine colored and he wore a kind of cloak of dark blue silk embroidered with silver thread. He had a hat of fur on his head and a regimental badge of two crossed sabres glittered from it.

The doctors stopped their work immediately and he said something to them in Russian. Then he came over to where Peter and I were sitting.

"I am Count Vinarsky of the Imperial Hussars," he said in excellent English. "I have come personally to congratulate you upon your charge. It was magnificent. I have never seen anything like it. My men are filled with wonderment and praise. But of course you were all drunk."

"Drunk?" cried Peter. "There hasn't been a man had a drink in the Tenth Hussars since the Alma a month ago."

"Impossible," cried the count. "I cannot believe it. Only men excited by liquor could face such odds."

The man with the heavily bandaged leg raised himself from his bed of straw on one elbow. "None of us had anything to drink," he said slowly. "I'll swear to it."

"How do you expect me to believe this?" the count asked. He was genuinely amazed. "Why

154

would men who are absolutely sober charge one battery of guns while running the gauntlet of two others?"

I thought of Corporal Baggins and the reply I made was really for him. "Because we were told to," I said. "That's why. We had our orders and we carried them out."

"But I could not get my own men to do such a thing," said the count. "There are no more spirited Hussars in Russia. But such a task as that? No! Never!" He said something in Russian to the doctors and there was a buzz of talk among them. The doctors looked at us as if we were mad.

"You tell me you are not drunk," the count said, "and so I must believe you." Another explanation seemed to occur to him for he said, "You must all be of the nobility then. That is it, eh? You are English noblemen who could not secure commissions and so enlisted as troopers."

"I'm just a poacher wanted in civil life for shooting a gamekeeper," said Peter.

"And I am not English," I added. "I'm Irish."

"Irish?" said the count turning to me with a look of interest.

"Yes."

"From what part of Ireland?"

"Galway."

"I have not yet had the pleasure of learning your name," said the Count.

"O'Connor," I replied. "Kevin O'Connor. Tenth Hussars."

"Indeed? That is very interesting." He clapped his hands and a man who must have been waiting outside entered with a tray upon which was a bottle and some glasses.

"I would be honored, gentlemen," he said, "if you would join me in a toast. A toast to a very gallant enemy." Peter and I and the man with the wounded leg, whose name was Streatham, drank with him. The poor fellow who had lost his arm was unconscious, and I believe died from lack of blood within the hour.

After this the count chatted with us for an hour very pleasantly indeed and promised that we would lack nothing for our comfort. We had scarcely eaten all day, and our breakfast, taken at dawn that morning, had been of salted pork. A fine meal was produced so that Peter remarked to me that maybe we weren't lords but we were certainly being treated as such.

The count then left and three cots were brought into the room. Heavy sheepskins were put over these and we were bedded down very comfortably indeed for the night. Things continued in this manner for two days.

The third day I got a fever from my wound and was not much aware of what was going on, for I would drop off into a coma for several hours at a time. I caught glimpses of Peter in my lucid moments sitting anxiously beside me, and I remained in this condition for a week and then began to mend.

When I was able to take a proper stock of things, Peter told me that Streatham had died. His leg had been shattered below the knee and he had developed gangrene. We were thus alone and although kindly treated and unguarded as far as Peter could find out, uncertain about our future. Count Vinarsky had not reappeared and our only visitors were two men who brought us food and cleaned up the room, and a doctor who came twice a day to check on me.

Peter did know where we were though. We were in a mansion belonging to the count about a mile north of Sebastopol. Part of the establishment was occupied by the count, part of it was used as a headquarters for his regiment, and the room we were in was a sort of hospital prison ward for prisoners of war.

"It seems strange that they should only have taken four of us," I said.

"They took more than that," said Peter. "There's about twenty others, I believe, in a hospital in Sebastopol."

"I wonder why we're being kept here then?" I asked.

Peter shrugged. "Maybe because we were captured by the count's regiment," he said. "We're like trophies. He doesn't want anyone else to have us."

On reflection I believe that was some part of the reason. But it was not all of it.

About a month after our capture, and when my wounds were mending well so that I was able to get about, though my arm was still in a splint, we received an invitation to dine with the count and his father. It was a surprising invitation for I was quite sure he had forgotten all about us. We had been given clothing to wear, and the evening of the dinner our uniforms were returned to us spotlessly clean and patched so beautifully that they seemed like new.

We were led to a small room whose walls of walnut panels glistened in the candlelight and there greeted by the count. He was full of apologies at not having seen us since the day of the famous charge, and explained that his military duties had kept him in the saddle night and day. He inquired after my health with genuine concern, and said that he had asked us to dine with him as his father had arrived from Petrograd and was most anxious, as an old cavalry man, to hear from our own lips the full story of the charge of the Light Brigade.

"The whole world," he said, "is still ringing with that famous exploit. I assure you that I would give all my lands and my titles to have taken part in it. You are fortunate among men—heroes in the classical sense of the word."

I gave Peter a slight kick for I suspected that he was about to reassert that he was a poacher who had killed a gamekeeper. Peter was of a practical turn of mind, not given to flights of fancy.

When the count's father, Prince Paul, arrived, I was immediately struck by his likeness to such pictures of the early saints as I had seen. He wore his hair long, down to his shoulders. It was gray and mingled in the most patriarchial manner with a full gray beard. I would judge by the age of his son that Prince Paul must have been a man in his sixties. And yet there was a twinkle to his eyes and a pinkness to his cheeks that belonged to a much younger man. Indeed, his face, despite its gravity, had a kind of boyishness to it.

We dined in the same room, an intimate circle of four, and the number of dishes served must have been a dozen, ranging from larks, roasted whole and served on a stick, to a sort of greenish mess of matter called caviar which was esteemed a great delicacy in Russia.

The talk was all of war, and the count deferred to his father, who told many tales of the Russian cavalry, dwelling particularly on actions in the Napoleonic War when he had been a young officer.

"But," he said, "I have never heard before of a cavalry charge such as that in which you two took part. It was for that reason that I instructed my son to keep you here, for I wanted a first-hand account of the adventure from beginning to end."

Peter looked at me, and I saw that I was elected to tell the tale. I gave all the details I could of the placement of the regiments, the belief that we were to charge the Turkish guns, the officer who had rushed to Lord Cardigan when the charge had started and been killed presumably before his message had been understood.

"In short," I concluded, "I believe that it was all a mistake and that we charged the wrong guns."

"Nonetheless you charged them," said the old Prince. "Now you have given me the tactical details. Tell me of your own feelings. I would like to live every second of that charge with you. Hold back nothing."

We had been served a quantity of vodka before our meal, and had wine to every dish, so that I felt an urge to talk, and so starting with the strange silence which had heralded our charge, and the remarkable cloud of mist which had enveloped the valley, I told them of all I had felt. Reference to the cloud of mist brought me to relating my story of the Foggy Dew and I told these two Russian noblemen, who listened with intense interest, the legend of the Foggy Dew, of my ancester Phelim O'Connor who had disappeared with the strange stone. I told them of my clashes with Lord Wedcomb and my hatred for him, and my conviction

160

that he was to be the agent of my death. I recounted my dream of the skeletons on the horses and how I had felt, at the latter end of the charge, that that nightmare had come true and I was living it.

In all this they did not interrupt with as much as a word. And when I had finished, there was a profound silence for several minutes.

"That," said the prince at last, "is the most remarkable tale I have ever heard in all my life. I came to hear the story of a cavalry charge, and I have been given a veritable romance."

"I had not intended to say so much," I said, dismayed at my openness with two strangers.

"We are indebted to you for a capital evening's entertainment," Prince Paul replied. "Indeed for more than that, as you shall discover later. But first why did you not kill or at least desert this Lord Wedcomb who has abused you so abominably? You had him at your mercy."

"I don't know why," I said.

"Then I shall tell you," said his highness. "It was precisely because you had him at your mercy. He was your enemy and you had mercy on him. You saved him. That is a very fine thing."

To this I said nothing.

"One thing more," the prince continued. "Do you know anything further of this ancestor of yours, this Phelim O'Connor who disappeared on

161

the hilltop in your homeland with the Foggy Dew?"

"No," I said. "And to tell you the truth I doubt sometimes that he ever existed."

"Not so fast," said the prince. "You may learn differently"

He rose and went to a small table which stood to one side of the room. It looked to me like a very fine writing table, a plain flat surface of walnut but without any drawers. He placed one of his hands on the top of the table, pressed down and pulled. And a fraction of an inch of the top slid aside revealing a cavity or container not more than the thickness of the table top below. When the prince returned to where we were sitting he had something in his hand. He held the clenched fist out to me and opened it swiftly.

"Would that be your Foggy Dew?" he asked.

In the palm of his hand was a stone as big as a walnut. It was as black as midnight. But in its depths emerald, gold, silver, and deep blue points of light flashed in the candlelight.

*

CHAPTER SEVENTEEN

PRINCE PAUL'S DRAMATIC PRODUCTION of the huge black opal, which glowed with constantly changing lights in the palm of his hand, left me for a while without a word which I could say. I looked at the stone incapable of crediting the evidence of my own eyes and then, without asking his permission, I picked it up in wonderment and awe.

"Where did you get this from?" I asked eventually.

"It has been in my family for over two centuries," his highness replied. "It is one of the oldest jewels we possess. Yet it does not belong to my family. We have been, shall I say, merely its guardians."

He took the stone from me and motioned me to a chair. Then he sat for a little while, looking at the gem with some affection, and said, "It is hard to know quite where to begin. Perhaps the best place would be with the arrival in Russia, some two hundred years ago, of a man with a strange name who came from, for us, a very remote part of the world. His name was Phelim O'Connor. And he came from Ireland."

"Phelim O'Connor?" I cried. "You mean my ancestor who disappeared."

"I would suspect that the two were the same," said the prince, "and I believe that this is the stone which you call the Foggy Dew.

"This man O'Connor would say nothing of his background to my people who then, as now, owned big estates in this part of Russia. He said merely that he was a soldier and that he came from Ireland and was seeking employment in the army of some prince or potentate in need of his services.

"Such a story may seem incredible today. But if you know anything of the history of your own country, you will realize that it was not an unusual situation two centuries ago. Many Irish gentlemen, forbidden to bear arms in their own country and to practice their faith, sold their swords and their services to the princes and kings of Europe from Sweden to Portugal. Phelim O'Connor came to my own ancestor, Prince Julian, with letters of high recommendation from both the French and Spanish armies. He had apparently served in both of them before making his way to Russia.

"I should mention that at that time our family estates were not in the Crimea, but around Moscow, where indeed the major portion of them are still located. It was not at all unusual that a European soldier-adventurer should come to Moscow seeking a commission in the army of some nobleman.

"Phelim O'Connor was given a commission in the army of my ancestor and he proved himself a soldier of outstanding ability. He brought with him many ideas, learned in France and Spain, for conducting sieges, provisioning soldiers, the proper use of cavalry and so on, which were entirely new to my country at the time. Added to this he had enormous personal courage. It was a favorite saying of his, still repeated in my family, that the best plans of a general are dependent upon the color of the private soldier's liver. To put spirit in his men, he was constantly in the place of danger, and achieved, finally, a rank equivalent to that of general.

"In all his time in Russia he never married nor spoke of marriage. Nor would he say very much about his background, except to discuss campaigns in which he had taken part as a professional soldier. It was presumed that he had left his native country, Ireland, because of some political situation and that in all probability he had a wife and a family there. But this was mere presumption. As I have said, he remained utterly secretive about these personal details.

"When he died, as a result of wounds sustained in a battle in our war against Sweden, Prince Julian was at his bedside. There was a strong affection between the two, unspoken perhaps, but very firm.

"Phelim O'Connor made a remarkable last request of the prince. He was proud all his life of his Irish blood, and he gave Prince Julian this stone which I now have in my hand. His request was that the family should keep the stone as its guardian. The stone was to be given to the man who filled the following three conditions.

"Firstly he must be an Irishman serving in a foreign army, as Phelim O'Connor had been himself.

"Secondly, that he must perform either an individual feat of enormous daring, or take part in an action in which the prospects of survival were of the slimmest.

"Thirdly he must spare the life of an enemy whom he hated and whom he had every opportunity to kill."

When he had concluded, the prince rose from his chair and came slowly towards me. "This dying wish of Phelim O'Connor's has been a charge upon my family for the last two centuries," he said. "It was a duty which we have many times despaired of ever discharging.

"When news reached Moscow of the charge of your Light Brigade, I was immediately interested as a cavalryman. But I scarcely think I would have come here, had not my son written to me of his conversation with you on the day of your capture."

"What conversation?" I asked.

"The conversation in which you identified yourself as an Irishman," replied the Prince. "It occurred to me immediately that here was an Irishman who had fulfilled two of the requirements to claim the stone which you call the Foggy Dew. In your talk tonight after dinner, when without any knowledge whatever even of my possession of the jewel, let alone the terms attached to it, you told the story of your hatred of Lord Wedcomb and your action in saving his life when you could have killed or deserted him, it became clear that you had fulfilled the third and final condition."

He looked once more at the stone, with a kind of affection and yet relief, and then put it in my hand.

"The Foggy Dew is yours," he said.

CHAPTER EIGHTEEN

The day after our dinner with Prince Paul and his son with its surprising climax, Peter and I were returned to the British lines in an exchange of prisoners. We would have been exchanged earlier, I found out, but were detained so that Prince Paul could interview me. We saw him only briefly before our departure and there was nothing I could say which was adequate to express my gratitude to him and my sense of bewilderment at having at last found and received the Foggy Dew.

To be sure, on the previous night we sat up for hours going over the story, speculating on the remarkable chance, which had resulted in myself, a descendant of Phelim O'Connor, receiving the jewel which might have gone to any other Irishman, whether a descendant of his or not, who fulfilled the conditions.

On this Prince Paul had this to say. "You call it a coincidence," he said, "and certainly it is. But is not life itself a series of astounding coincidences? A cavalryman's horse stumbles upon a stone, or perhaps falters in its stride and a ball aimed directly for the rider misses. Or one which was not aimed at him, kills him. Who is to calculate what are the odds of such a thing happening? Yet such occurrences are the commonplaces of battle. We accept them knowing only that they do happen."

After that I felt less astounded at receiving the Foggy Dew and even came to think that it was quite as surprising that of the thousands of cannon shot which had thundered down the valley of Balaclava, many so close that a few inches to left or right and I would have been struck, none had killed me. For his part Peter had a theory of his own.

"I don't believe that story of Phelim O'Connor," he said. "I think the old prince made it all up. You told him of the story of the Foggy Dew describing it as a black opal. He had taken a fancy to you and decided to give you a black opal which belonged to his own family. He knew you wouldn't accept the gift so he just elaborated on your tale and made it look as though the opal belonged to you."

This was a new approach indeed. I cannot say that I accepted it. But it was certainly something to think about.

When we got back to our own lines I learned that Lord Wedcomb was still alive and had returned to England. We ourselves were sent home on the first hospital ship which left—myself because my wounded arm made me useless for active service, and Peter because he had a return of dysentery which incapacitated him.

Throughout the long voyage home, during which time, though wounded myself, I was employed as a nurse to the hundreds of more seriously wounded men jammed in the holds of the hospital ship, I wondered what I should do when I returned to Dublin.

I now had, in the Foggy Dew, money with which to buy a sufficient acreage of land to make my mother and myself independent of landlords for life. But there was still the question of the charges against me. As soon as I was out of the army I would have to stand trial on these charges. I tormented myself with worries about being convicted and with concern that as a felon, whatever property I had might be confiscated. I debated giving the stone to Peter so that he could pretend that it was his property. But he quickly pointed out that he was wanted as much as I and that if the property of felons was automatically confiscated, then the stone would be taken from him also.

It was an agonizing position to be in—to have in my pocket sufficient to ensure my ease and that of my mother for the rest of my life, and at the same time to be faced with the prospect of being sentenced to the prison hulks or transported to a penal colony the minute I obtained a discharge from the army.

Eventually I decided upon a step which seemed completely desperate. I would go to Lord Wedcomb and ask him to withdraw the charges against me. He had the power to do so, though I had hardly a hope that he would. I had saved him at Balaclava. But his lordship, from what I knew of his character, would regard that as merely my duty as his inferior. He was not likely to be grateful for it.

We reached Dublin a year after we had sailed and my application for leave was granted as much because of my part in the charge as because of my wounds. I also received my pay, which totaled some thirty pounds, and learned that Lord Wedcomb had gone to country estates in Galway.

At that my heart failed me. To return to the very place where I was wanted as a fugitive seemed to me the heighth of foolishness. I might well be arrested before I got to see Lord Wedcomb. I decided to seek a lawyer and ask his advice, and in this received some assistance from Lieutenant Greaves who put me in touch with a Mr. Penrith with offices in a musty building on Sackville Street.

"He's as honest as it is possible for a lawyer to be," he said. "But there is this to be said for him—his practice is small and therefore he is hungry and in need of clients. He will do what he can for you and take all he can."

This was no great recommendation. And when I first met Mr. Penrith I was not at all impressed with him. His office was a tumbled down cupboard of a room, the planks which formed the floor being bare and rutted with wear so that the knots in the wood stood out upon them like so many boils.

Not much of this floor was to be seen, however, for it was piled high with stacks of documents, their edges covered with dust and yellowed with time. Seated behind a rickety table among these cliffs of papers, with an ancient goosequill behind his ear, was Mr. Penrith. He had a set of dentures upon the desk before him, and as I entered he put these in his mouth, explaining without any show of embarrassment that they had belonged to his father, and though he had been wearing them ten years, they still hurt his gums.

"What can I do for you?" he asked in a voice which had the querulous note of a door—long unused—being opened.

I did not know how much I could tell a stranger of my story and had the layman's distrust of lawyers. So I pretended that I had come on behalf of a friend who had got into trouble but obtained some property and now wanted to clear himself with the law. I gave the details of the trouble, telling my own story, but attributing it to my mythical friend.

Mr. Penrith listened with a look of complete boredom. He kept working his mouth at the discomfort of his dentures and rapped a little tattoo, while I was talking, with his fingernails upon the table top as if anxious that I should finish.

"You say," he squeaked, "that you are charged with an attack upon the person of Lord Wedcomb and inciting the peasantry to riot?"

"Not I," I said. "My friend."

"Sir," said Mr. Penrith, "I put it to you that you and your friend are one and the same person."

"I'm afraid you're right," I said meekly.

"It's a remarkable thing," continued Mr. Penrith, "but with lawyers, people ask their advice but insist that it is needed for a friend. The public has a peculiar distrust of the law, confusing the legal profession with the constabulary. The two are not the same.

"Now," he continued. "Have you seen any of these charges published?"

"You mean printed notices saying that I am wanted?" I asked.

"I do not," snapped Mr. Penrith. "I mean have you ever seen or heard of a warrant for your arrest as a fugitive from justice."

"No."

"Do you know whether such a warrant exists?"

"No."

"Have you ever taken steps to inquire whether such a warrant exists?"

"No. I ran. They would have killed me."

"Did anyone ever tell you that such a warrant existed?"

"Only Tom of the Three Fingers. He said if I was handed over to the civil authorities I would certainly be tried and sentenced."

"Did it ever occur to you that this person called Tom of the Three Fingers had good reasons for wanting you to believe such a thing—that he needed a dupe who could be frightened into an attempt to assassinate Lord Wedcomb as part of the terrorist movement of the Young Irelanders?"

That stopped me. Such a thought had never occurred to me before. "No," I said. "I never thought of that."

"Hah," said Mr. Penrith. "Let me put that more clearly for you. You never thought at all. You just ran.

"Now," he continued, "our first task is to discover whether you are indeed wanted on any or all of these charges. Mind you I don't say that you are and I don't say that you are not. I say merely that the point has not been determined. That will require a search. And a search requires a fee." He hesitated, took the ancient goosequill from behind his ears, and examined the end of it without interest.

"The fee will be two pounds, payable in advance," he said to the end of the goosequill.

I gave him the two pounds readily enough, placing the gold coins on the table. He looked at them as if they were not of the slightest interest to him.

"Come back tomorrow," he said. "I give you a good day, sir." It was two steps to the door, and I saw out of the tail of my eye that he pocketed the two sovereigns before I reached it.

The next day I was early at Mr. Penrith's office —too early in fact. He said he had not yet completed his search and that I should come back that afternoon at four. I spent the day in an agony, torn between hope and despair, and walked about the city to keep myself occupied. Once I found myself in precisely the same part of Phoenix Park where I had lain in ambush waiting for Lord Wedcomb's coach. I almost ran from the place.

When at last four o'clock came and I returned to Mr. Penrith's office he was not there, and I waited for perhaps an hour before he put in his appearance.

"Well, young sir," he said, "I have made a search of all the warrants on record issued at the time of your—ahem, misfortunes—and I find none concerning you. However," he continued, "this evidence is indicative, not conclusive. To make sure, it will be necessary for me to get in touch with Lord Wedcomb and ascertain whether he ever swore out a warrant for your arrest on any kind of a charge."

"How long will that take?" I asked.

"That I cannot say," said Mr. Penrith. "It will depend entirely upon his lordship's graciousness in replying to my letter. It might be two weeks. It might be two months. It might possibly be longer."

"I can't wait that long," I said. "I will go to Lord Wedcomb myself."

And so I did. I bought a horse and made the journey to Galway in three days. I will never forget the mixed emotions which arose when I again came in sight of Spaniard's Hill and saw the place where our little cabin had once stood. There was no trace of the cabin. The whole area was now devoted to pasture and cows stood grazing where once we had had our potato patch. My heart hardened at the sight and the old black anger and hatred of Lord Wedcomb and the privilege he stood for returned to me. When I got to the door of his big mansion, these feelings had reached such a peak of intensity that I found myself breathing hard and trembling slightly.

The door was opened by his butler, who looked me over with great disfavor and inquired my name and business. I said I was Trooper O'Connor of the Tenth Hussars and wished to see his lordship.

"You should use the servant's entrance," said the butler. "It is around to the side," and proceeded to close the door.

Then I heard Lady Barbara call from inside, "Who is it, Johnson?"

"A soldier, your Ladyship," said Johnson. "By the name of O'Connor."

"Let him in," she said and when the door opened, she was standing in the hallway.

Her first words to me were, "You are alive. We thought you were dead. Lord Wedcomb said you fell wounded from your horse behind the Russian guns."

"I was captured," I replied.

"My brother owes you his life," she said softly. "I am glad you didn't die."

She led me into a reception room to one side of the hall and motioned me to be seated.

"Do you remember that night on the banks of the Danube, the night you killed the Cossack and saved me?" she asked. "Do you remember I asked you whether you would have saved my brother and you said no?"

"Yes," I said. "I remember."

"You did save him though," she continued. "You said you wouldn't and yet you did. You are a strange man, Kevin O'Connor."

To this I said nothing, for there was nothing to be said.

"Why have you come here?" she asked.

"To see your brother."

"I will get him for you." She went and was back in a little while with Lord Wedcomb. He had the same imperious look, the same superior attitude and voice. "Ah, O'Connor," he said. "I hadn't expected to see you again. What is your business, pray?"

"My Lord," I said, "I have come to discover whether you have issued any charges against me."

"Charges?" he said. "Charges?"

"For my attack upon you, and for inciting to riot," I answered dully.

"Nonsense," said his lordship. "Do you suppose that a man of my position would appear in court and testify that a mere. . . ." He stopped himself with a great effort.

"O'Connor," he said, "I am greatly indebted to you for my own life and that of my sister. I have no charges to make against you. I . . . er . . . I . . . er."

"Charles means that he would like to thank you and shake your hand," said Lady Barbara.

He looked at her astounded and outraged. "Yes," he said. "Damn, I suppose I do." He held out a hand as limp as a dead fish and I took it.

"I called you coward once," said his lordship. "Forgive me. I was wrong." I believe it cost him as much courage to say that as it had to lead his regiment into the Russian guns at Balaclava.

CHAPTER NINETEEN

FROM THE SALE OF THE FOGGY DEW I received ten
thousand pounds. With this sum I bought twenty
acres of land, including the land my mother and I
had previously rented. Where our little cabin of
turf had stood I built a stone cottage which looked
to us like a palace.

My mother had spent the year of my absence
with Mr. Forster as his housekeeper. I was much
indebted to him, for though he had paid her nothing, it being most painful for him to part with
money, he had provided her with food and shelter.
She had been without news of me except for a visit
from Tom of the Three Fingers, who had in-
formed her that I had joined the army, but made
no mention of his efforts to frighten me into as-
sassinating Lord Wedcomb.

Our life in our new house went forward with a
kind of happiness and serenity which we had never
previously dreamed of, and I thought often of
how Tom of the Three Fingers had said that I
might be the one to find the Foggy Dew, but
would have to go through a period of great trial

179

and hardship first. Certainly that part of his prophecy had come true. And yet I sometimes wondered whether Peter's version of the jewel had not been correct, namely that Prince Paul had wished to make me some kind of a gift, and had merely elaborated on my own story in order to give me the black opal. At times I believed that this was the case. And at other times, it seemed that so much of the story of Tom of the Three Fingers had come about that the legend of the jewel was certainly true.

In the end I became very confused, and did not know which to believe.

But in recounting all this I am somewhat ahead of my story. After discovering from Lord Wedcomb that he had laid no charges against me, and having a joyful reunion with my mother in which I related all my adventures and the good fortune which had come my way, I had to return to my regiment in Dublin.

My period of service, however, was not long, for the Crimean War coming finally to a close, both Peter and I received our discharges. Peter was for taking service on board a ship, being afraid of remaining in Ireland because of the charge of killing the gamekeeper which had been laid against him. But I convinced him that he must face this charge, for he could not spend the rest of his life running away from it.

We engaged Mr. Penrith as Peter's lawyer and

that strange gentleman expressed delight that the charge against Peter was one of willful murder.

"Nothing could be better," he squeaked. "If found guilty you will certainly be hanged. Manslaughter would be bad. But willful murder? I declare it excellent."

Both the charge and Mr. Penrith's attitude threw Peter and me into a state of panic. But the remarkable lawyer knew what he was doing. During the trial he seemed to delight in emphasizing the gravity of the offense of willful murder and extolled the sentence of hanging which was mandatory. He denounced all murderers in fiercest terms and praised the portion of the law which fixed the death sentence for them.

To be sure, he brought out the fact that Peter and the gamekeeper had quarreled and it was with the gamekeeper's gun that the latter had been killed. But he did not attempt much else in the matter of defense, and as the prosecution built up its case, pointing to Peter's previous record as a poacher, the bad blood which had existed between Peter and the gamekeeper, and produced a witness who testified that Peter had said all gamekeepers should be shot like vermin, things looked black indeed.

Mr. Penrith made only a short address to the jury. He praised once again the British system of justice, complimented the prosecution on their conduct of the case and then said:

"Willful murder means planned murder. It demands that the culprit bring with him a lethal weapon with which to execute the victim. But I tell you gentlemen, that the only time my client ever had a lethal weapon in his hand with intent to kill was when he drew his sword in the cause of his Queen, and charged the Russian gunners at Balaclava with the Light Brigade."

That did it. Throughout the trial no mention had been made of Peter's part in that charge. The jury without even retiring pronounced Peter "Not Guilty," and several of the jurymen helped carry him from the court in a procession of triumph.

Not much now remains to be told. Peter came with me to Galway, and took to fishing (and I believe smuggling). I met once again Mr. Neal and his daughter Kathleen who had rescued me the night our cabin had been destroyed.

My feelings toward Mr. Neal were mixed. He had saved my life. Yet there was the suspicion that he had done so merely to use me as a tool. I tackled him squarely on the subject at our first meeting, asking him whether he had known of the plot to assassinate Lord Wedcomb with me as the assassin.

"Yes," he said. "I knew that an attempt to kill Lord Wedcomb was to be made. It was I who gave the order. But I didn't know that Tom of the Three Fingers had tried to make you the assassin or fix the blame on you. Not," he added, "that it would have made any difference to me."

"Then why did you save me at all—why did you send your daughter Kathleen to the top of Spaniard's Hill to lead me to the cave and then get me away to the French schooner?"

"I answered that before," said Mr. Neal. "It was because you had made a stand. If you made a stand and were killed, others would lose courage. If you made a stand and escaped, others would be encouraged to follow your lead.

"There's got to be an end to this business in Ireland of rich landlords and impoverished tenants with no chance of buying land of their own. The problem is solved for you. But it still exists for the rest of the tenants around here." That is all Mr. Neal would say.

On the Wedcomb estates in Galway, and largely through the influence of Lady Barbara, the problem was solved earlier than for the rest of Ireland. Lord Wedcomb cut out all the intermediates who existed between him and his tenants. He rented his land directly to the tenant's, and this brought about a great reduction in their rents since the profits of middlemen were eliminated. Furthermore, he agreed that a portion of the rental would be devoted towards purchase of the land, and although it might take a family three generations to buy their small acreage, nonetheless they had the prospect of eventually owning it outright—something for which they had never hoped before.

As for Kathleen, the beautiful shy girl who had saved me on Spaniard's Hill and visited me in the terrible days in the cave, I saw more and more of her and fell more and more in love with her until the day came that we were married.

And prominent among the wedding guests was Tom of the Three Fingers. He came over the top of Spaniard's Hill one day, a week before my wedding, dressed the same as he had the day of the start of my adventures.

"Top of the morning," he called out, as soon as he had caught sight of me, and continued on with the greatest ease and cheeriness about the weather and the crop prospects and the places he had been, as if there was no cause in the world for any strain between us.

At first I was outraged at him for a hypocrite and a rascal and a man who had endangered my life with his assassination plot while posing all the time as my friend. When I charged him with treachery and perfidy, he was silent a while, seated upon the sack which he always carried and staring moodily at the ground.

"There's no gratitude in the human race at all," he said at length.

"Gratitude!" I cried. "You tried to pin a murder on me and you talk of gratitude?"

"Me boy," said Tom, "will ye look a minute at

the facts and when you have looked at them, you'll bless the day that the good Lord set me upon the earth and caused us to meet.

"Wasn't it I who told you of the Foggy Dew and of the trials you must endure to find it? Wasn't it I who was the cause of your joining the army? And wasn't it as a result of joining the army that you eventually found the stone as the prophecy had foretold? And wasn't it as a result of all this that your present happiness has come, with you to be wedded in a week to the darlingest girl in the whole length and breadth of the land?— may God preserve her."

"Yes," I said. "But your intentions were quite different. Your intentions were to assassinate Lord Wedcomb and then pin the deed upon me."

"Intentions!" he cried with the greatest scorn. "What is the value of intentions? Are not we all the instruments of our Creator, and wasn't it my humble part upon this earth to bring about all this happiness for you? Added to which," he concluded, "I have brought you a salmon."

I think it was the mention of the salmon that did it. I laughed. There was nothing to be done with such a rascal but accept him and so he came with us to our house and remained as a wedding guest, full of the brightest stories of happenings around the country that have ever been told.

On the Foggy Dew I questioned him a great deal, telling him Peter's version of the gaining of the stone and asking him his opinion as to which had been true—the legend or the theory which Peter had devised.

Finally he lost his patience with me and said, "Me boy, believe whichever you want. It's a matter of your state of mind. There's some who believe in legends and some who are always looking for explanations and so will never be happy. For myself, I find it impossible to believe that a Russian Prince should give a private soldier a jewel worth ten thousand pounds just out of the kindness of his heart.

"Where is the Foggy Dew now?" he asked.

"It is with the Dublin jeweler to whom I sold it some months ago," I replied.

"There have been some queer mists in Dublin these past weeks," said Tom speculatively. "They've come out of the sea like ghosts coming from their graves and they've been colder than an unburied corpse."

I left him then for I could see that he was busy with another legend.